TWILIGHT
BOY

TWILIGHT BOY

by Timothy Green

rising moon
Books for Young Readers from Northland Publishing

For Shundiin—my ray of sunlight.
And for Dazhoni, my beautiful one.

The cover illustration was rendered in acrylic on illustration board
The text type was set in Adobe Garamond
The display type was set in Meridian
Composed in the United States of America
Designed by Rudy J. Ramos
Cover designed by Billie Jo Bishop
Edited by Susan Tasaki
Editorial Direction by Tom Carpenter
Production supervised by Lisa Brownfield
Composed and manufactured in the United States of America

FIRST IMPRESSION
ISBN 0-87358-670-0 (hc)
ISBN 0-87358-640-9 (sc)

Library of Congress Catalog Card Number 97-49958
Green, Timothy, date.
Twilight boy / by Timothy Green.
p.   cm.
Summary: Jesse Begay begins to investigate the strange circumstances
surrounding a fire at his Navajo grandfather's hogan, even though the
old man remains convinced that a "skinwalker" is haunting him.
ISBN 0-87358-670-0. — ISBN 0-87358-640-9 (pbk.)
[1. Mystery and detective stories. 2. Navajo Indians—Fiction. 3. Indians
of North America—New Mexico—Fiction. 4. Horses— Fiction.]   I. Title.
PZ7.G82636Tw 1998

[Fic]—dc21   97-49958

613/3.5M/2-98 (sc)
613/2M/2-98 (hc)

There is flash-lightning in their mouths,
With their voices they are calling me,
Dark music sounds from their mouths,
With their voices they are calling me,
They call out into the dawn,
With their voices they are calling me,
Their voices reach all the way out to me,
With their voices they are calling me.

—Navajo Chant

ACKNOWLEDGMENTS

I wish to acknowledge my debt to David Seppa, whose keen pen cut through the early draft of this story. I also wish to thank Susan Tasaki for her fine editing, and Erin Murphy and Tom Carpenter at Northland, for their valued input and know-how extraordinaire.

AUTHOR'S NOTE

The characters and events in this book are purely fictitious. Red Rock Trading Post does not exist, nor do a number of places I describe on Ramah Navajo Reservation. I borrowed names for the setting from all over the reservation.

El Morro, on the other hand, is quite real, and the history surrounding Coronado's search for gold is accurate. And yes, skinwalkers abound throughout the reservation, at least in myth and rumor.

PART I
Day/White

CHAPTER ONE

The darkest secrets are often buried like old bones, and only their ghosts, their *chindi* speak aloud. Harrison Chee tipped the bottle of whiskey to his lips one final time . . . empty. Like so much of the past.

After all this time, after all the curing ceremonies, there was still no harmony. No *hózhó*. He tried to set the bottle down, but it escaped his fingers, bounced off the edge of the table, and landed with a soft thud on the dirt floor. No *hózhó*.

Old emotions welled up—the grief, the fear—but they were now so expected, so familiar, that even their melancholy was comforting.

He awkwardly picked up the coin lying on the table. Rubbing his eyes with the back of a shirtsleeve, he thought about where it came from. Minutes passed while his memory wandered in the past. *Why?* he wondered, carefully replacing the tarnished gold piece on the table. Like an amber eye, it stared up at him; inflicting wounds that bled in the deepest recesses of his heart. His vision blurred.

Staggering to his feet, Chee moved unsteadily toward the wooden chest huddled in the darkest corner of the small hogan. A smear of light from the single lantern caused his shadow to move ahead of him with giant steps and then leap out from the dirty, unadorned gypsum-board wall. The key to the chest had disappeared long ago; its latch now hung loose, freed from the lock by a crowbar many years earlier. Chee rummaged through his valuables until he found it: a small cardboard box tied with a criss-cross of string. With difficulty he unfastened it, dropped the box lid into the chest, and returned to the table, tottering like a stack of kindling sticks balanced in a windstorm.

Sitting down heavily, he dumped the contents onto the table and examined them: an expired driver's license; a silver-and-turquoise bracelet that had been his father's; an ancient wedding photo of himself as a young man and Delbah, his bride; and his *jish* bundle, containing an arrowhead, two stone fetishes—one of an owl, the other of a turtle, a bear's claw, and a clear plastic prescription vial containing a few flecks of sacred corn pollen. Next to the *jish* bundle was the evil talisman . . . the coin. An exact duplicate of the one on the table. Same size, same worn images: a lion emblazoned on a shield, and the portraits of three kings. Same faded writing.

Chee knew these coins. They were the gold pieces that had caused the ghost sickness that had infected his younger brother, had caused him to die. They were the same coins he had buried with his brother sixty years ago. As a boy, Chee had tucked them into the soft folds of his brother's coffin, ensuring that the treasure had been returned to the dead from whence it came.

And now the *chindi* were playing a game with him. The first coin had been returned about a year ago, placed at his doorstep sometime during the night. The second one was left only last night. Maybe the spirits were calling to him, directing him to return the coins to where they had been found, or maybe it was simply a cruel joke, a sure way to torture the guilty one still living.

Chee couldn't breathe.

Somehow managing to make it to the door, he pushed it open to the night. The air was chilling. A lone moth dodged past, darted toward the lantern, and spun around and around the light. Chee peered up at the sky, trying not to lose his balance. A full moon shone overhead; stars glittered by the thousands, almost close enough to touch. From the darkness, a breeze whispered through the scattering of piñon and juniper, rustled a tattered piece of tar paper on the dilapidated hogan. He propped himself against the door frame and looked out, allowing the night air to soothe his senses.

In front of Chee, the old plank storage shack and a brush arbor, which offered shade during the summer months, stood in silhouette near a cluster of cedar. Just over the arroyo, the sheep pen stood empty. He was glad of that. All the sheep were up at Spencer Tsosie's summer hogan. Let Tsosie take care of them for awhile. Besides, his brother-in-law owed him money, and Chee knew he'd never see a dime of it. Might as well let Tsosie work it off.

Ever since Marshaw had married him, some forty years ago, the man had been a weight around Chee's neck. Always needed to borrow money. Tsosie had an aunt—an ancient woman whom relatives say used to be a crystal gazer—a woman with strong medicine. Let him

3

borrow money from her from now on. Ironically, after the old woman lost her sight, her visions had grown even clearer, some said. But he heard she had retired: too many problems with relatives who never paid. The thought made Chee smile. That's relatives for you.

The night shadows moved slightly. Chee stared until his eyes watered; he rubbed them and stared some more.

Nothing.

The booze was playing tricks on him. He started to close the door but thought he caught a glimpse of something. Something running with silent swiftness across a patch of moonlight. It disappeared behind a growth of bushes not fifty feet away.

Whatever it was, it made the hair on the back of his neck bristle. Maybe it was one of the stray dogs that kept getting into his garbage at night. Or maybe it was one of those witches who can turn into a wolf, a skin-walker. Hadn't he thought he saw one last year? Right around the time he received the first gold coin. Maybe a witch was stirring things up with the dead. Chee recalled how he'd been followed by a coyote last week, and he knew it had been a messenger from the Holy People, a sign of impending danger. He glanced back at the old Wilbur Hauck single-shot .22 propped against the wall. Well, just let it try coming in.

He shut the door.

It was probably only a skunk, Chee told himself as he sat down on the cot. Booze always made him edgy. The cinders in the wood stove that occupied the center of the room glowed comfortingly. He was tired. Pulling off his clothes with an effort, Chee turned down the

4

flame in the kerosene lantern and lay down on the cot's rumpled sheets. Only a skunk, he repeated to himself. He was out of breath but felt sober now. Stretching, he pulled a cigarette from the pack stashed under the mattress, found matches tucked in the cellophane wrapper, and lit it. He propped his head up for comfort and recalled the stories his grandfather had told him many years ago

Monster Slayer, the son of Changing Woman, had made the land safe for the *Diné*, the People. He had killed all the monsters, and he was coming home when he met someone who would still prey on the inhabitants of the earth. "I thought I killed all the enemies of the People. Where did you come from?"

"My name is Poverty. If you destroy me, then you will be the one who destroys humanity, my grandchild. You see, the People will have no knowledge of need, or the necessity of helping one another. If you kill me, the People will be like the rest of the animal world; they will have no compassion for one another. If you kill me, the People will be like the rest of the animal world; they will have no compassion for their fellow man."

So Monster Slayer did not kill Poverty. Next, he came across another stranger . . .

Outside, a shape half-hidden by piñons stood up in the night's shadow. He watched the light beneath the hogan's east-facing door grow dimmer and waited. The stars called to him. The moon spoke his name. He knew patience. The sweet smell of burning cedar drifted from the hogan and touched him.

He was like the smoke. Quiet. Formless. Deadly.

A wolf skin draped his shoulders loosely, the forepaws on his chest. He wore the wolf's empty skull on his head, the snout pointed upward, as if it were silently howling in the night. He *was* the wolf whose skin he wore.

An owl hooted. A sign. He crept closer.

Like a shadowdancer, the wolf circled the hogan. He stopped and peered through the small window, then smiled. The old fool had fallen asleep with a cigarette still in his hand. A long gray ash balanced between the old man's fingers as he lay with his arms crossed over himself; his chest moved up and down in gentle rhythm. For a moment the wolf felt a tinge of sorrow for the destruction that was soon to follow. But it was fleeting. Terror had its purpose.

In the darkness, a sudden flash of light revealed a match held to a strip of cloth. The material, saturated with kerosene, burned hungrily. It dangled like a fiery tongue from the glass jar filled with more of the flammable liquid. The wolf let the rag burn to the jar's very lip before he stepped back and tossed it lightly toward Chee's brush arbor.

The cedar poles and brush roof went up in a roar of white flame. The wolf stepped back to the edge of the piñons, shielding his eyes with one hand as he watched the inferno. Even where he stood, the heat was nearly overpowering. Giant flames licked at the dark sky; glowing red cinders swarmed upward. It was beautiful, he thought. The crackling wood hissed and popped. Smoke, black as the darkest of evil, pirouetted toward the stars.

Harrison Chee tumbled out of his hogan, an

expression of horror on his face. He hoisted the old rifle to his shoulder and aimed at the thing standing less than thirty yards away. "Get away from here, you devil," he stammered.

The wolf smiled.

"I mean it," Chee warned. "I'll shoot."

The wolf laughed.

Chee fired. A flash erupted from the trembling barrel; the report thundered in his ears, numbing his senses. He fell backward. Terror-stricken, Chee turned away—but then he had to look. . . .

The wolf had disappeared.

CHAPTER TWO

Jesse Begay slid off his horse and stood near the smoldering ash of what used to be his grandfather's brush arbor. Behind the charred ruins, the hogan stood as lone sentinel. He noticed there wasn't any sign of life from inside the dwelling; its windows were as black and empty as skull sockets. Nothing moved. Nothing except the eddy of wind that whistled through the piñons, dusting small puffs of gray ash onto his tennis shoes.

He seemed not to notice. His eyes traveled across the debris, glanced at the empty sheep pens, then moved on to the sun-bleached truck sitting on cinderblocks in the weeds. A scrawny rooster shaded himself beneath its hulk, bobbing his head up and down as he pecked at something in the sand.

Tying his horse's reins to a fencepost, the boy approached the hogan. The door suddenly opened and out stepped the old man, shielding his eyes from the sun's glare with one hand, holding a rifle in the other.

The boy spoke to him in Navajo: *"Haash iínidzan?"* What happened?

"Hóla." I don't know.

The boy frowned.

Harrison Chee shook his head and turned back toward his shack. End of discussion.

"Daashínít'é, What's wrong," he asked his grandfather.

"Ádin. Ni wodina nina." Nothing. Just stay away.

Ignoring the rebuff, he followed his grandfather inside and sat down on the crackled vinyl sofa, adjusting himself to fit the lumpy cushion. The old man seated himself on the one wooden chair that didn't teeter. His face was oddly blank, the boy noticed, as if life had drained out of it and all that was left was emptiness. It saddened him to see his grandfather this way.

The old man was slowly wasting away, the boy realized. His grandfather's gray hair, tied back with a dirty red bandanna, was dry and lifeless; his thin eyelids had a bruised and shiny look, and on his nose and cheeks were the burst capillaries of a life-long drinker.

The room was dark and smelled of smoke and booze.

"You have to tell me what happened," the boy said, switching to English. "How did it burn down?"

"How?" his grandfather repeated. "Very quickly."

The grandson smiled thinly. "Were you drunk last night?"

"That's a foolish question. I'm drunk every night."

"Why the gun, Grandfather? Who do you plan on shooting?"

"You, if you don't quit asking so many questions."

The boy reached over and picked up the antique .22, sniffed the barrel, and recognized the sulfuric smell of gunpowder; it had been fired recently. He opened the

9

cylinder chamber and removed the new cartridge. Harrison Chee watched indifferently. He had more.

"What do you want me to do, throw the bullets at 'em instead?"

"At who?"

"Yee naaldlooshii." The skinwalker.

The boy looked up at him, unsure what to say, what to think. "You saw one?"

"Of course I saw one. I tried to shoot him." Harrison Chee stared out the window. "But he disappeared."

The boy followed the old man's gaze out toward the smoldering remains of the brush arbor. "So you saw someone do this?"

"Not *someone*. The witch."

"How do you know it was a witch?"

"Because I saw him."

"What did he look like?"

"A witch."

"You're impossible."

Chee looked at his grandson. "And you're a smart-mouthed kid," he said, "who thinks he knows more than his elders."

As the boy stood up, he noticed that some of the confusion had left the old man's eyes. "I'm going to go look around. Then I think we should call the police."

"Sure. We'll use my phone."

"Funny. I'll call from the trading post. Where are your sheep?"

Chee pointed out to nowhere in particular. "Tsosie has 'em. He's probably lost half the herd by now. He's got the laziest dogs; they'd let a coyote come up and snatch a lamb

10

without even barking. It's because he hardly feeds 'em."

"I'll go check for tracks," the boy offered, anxious not to hear the story about Tsosie's dogs again. "I'd like to see if there are any prints out there besides mine and those of an old man staggering around taking pot shots at trees and anything else he sees moving."

"You sass me just like your mother does. First, come over here and sit down, Jesse. I want to show you something." Chee patted the chair next to him and then held out a small shoe box. "Sit here and open it."

Reluctantly, Jesse sat down again. "What is it?"

"Open it."

Jesse pulled off the lid, peered inside, then dumped the contents onto the table. What immediately caught his eye were the two gold coins that rolled toward the table's edge.

"Where did you get these?" he said, stopping both coins with his hand.

"Nazhoni." They're beautiful, aren't they?

"Aó." Where did you get them?

"They were given to me."

The boy looked up at Chee, his brow raised inquisitively, waiting.

Chee enjoyed this part: "From the *chindi*. The coins are gifts from the dead."

Jesse was silent. He looked down at the coins and waited for his grandfather to tell him more, knowing it was important that he showed patience, allowed the old man to tell his story at his own pace, in his own way.

Chee continued after a calculated pause. "When I was a young boy, around your age, I did something

11

terrible. These coins—I stole them . . . but the *chindi,* they saw, and they brought death. I later returned the coins to the land of the dead, but as you can see, the *chindi* have given them back. Maybe they're playing games with this old man, or maybe they're telling me to return them to Broken Bones; I don't know."

"What do you mean, the *chindi* gave them back?" Jesse asked. "How? And when? Who's Broken Bones?"

Harrison Chee raised a hand, silencing him. "Listen. Don't interrupt with your impatience. 'Who? How? When?' I'm telling you. Don't confuse me." Chee studied his steepled fingers. "Where was I?"

"You said the *chindi* gave you back the coins," the boy offered. "When?"

Chee scowled. "The first one was given to me a year ago. The second one was given to me last night. Or was it the night before? . . . I can't remember."

"You mean an evil spirit walked up and handed them to you?" Jesse asked, aware of the sarcasm in his tone.

Chee noticed it, too. He glowered at his grandson. "Of course not. The coins were left at my doorstep during the night. Maybe the skinwalker brought them. Those witches can communicate with ghosts, you know."

"Grandfather, you said something about the *chindi* had brought death. Whose death?"

"I cannot speak his name. But I loved him."

The boy nodded his understanding. It was a Navajo taboo to speak the name of a dead person; it could cause its *chindi* to come to you. But his grandfather had said "I cannot speak *his* name." It might be the old man's

12

younger brother, what was his name? Tyrone. He remembered his father once telling him something about the brother, about the old man's undying grief for Tyrone. So it was all tied into that, he mused. The fire, as well as his grandfather's ramblings, were making even less sense. "Who's Broken Bones?" Jesse asked, certain that he was losing more of the old man's attention by the minute.

"Who?"

"Broken Bones."

Chee shook his head. *"Hóla."* He stood up with an effort, still wagging his head back and forth. "I'm going to make some coffee. You go look for tracks." End of discussion.

Puzzled, the boy watched as his grandfather shuffled over to the jug of water near the stove. He carefully returned the coins to the old man's small collection of valuables, then stood up and headed toward the door. "I'll be back in a bit," he called over his shoulder. There was no acknowledgment from the old man. The sunlight seemed to swallow him as he cupped his hand over his eyes, waiting for them to adjust to the brightness. Overhead, the crystalline blue sky shimmered; there were no clouds to soften its intensity. Jesse stooped close to the ground and studied the red, trampled earth.

His own tracks were the easiest to make out: His soles left tiny circular imprints in the sand. His grandfather's smooth, worn prints were no trouble to identify either. The left heel mark was deeper on the outside, revealing a heel worn unevenly; the old man needed to see a cobbler. His grandfather's steps were also short, with toes pointed outward: telltale signs of a bowlegged person. The tracks patterned the ground to and from the remains of the brush arbor to the outhouse out back and over to the sheep pens. His father had taught him how to read tracks, had even shown him how to tell which direction a man or an animal was traveling when the tracks were nothing but flattened spots of grass. Look at the direction of the bent blades of grass, son. A man's step will push the blades forward—that's how we walk. An animal's steps will bend the grass backward. The memory tugged at his heart. His father would've known what to make of this. He would've come up with a logical explanation.

Near the cinders, the boy's eyes caught a glimpse of something foreign. He sucked in his breath and looked closer. There it was: a fresh print made by someone other than his grandfather or himself. It was smooth like his grandfather's, but the heel was flat, the toe more rounded.

There were more. Tracks led to the hogan, to the windows, and then back again. Tracks backed away from the brush arbor, turned, headed toward the trees. They were large prints, maybe size eleven or twelve boots. A big man. And there was a crack in the sole of the right boot, near the arch. Excitement sparked in Jesse's chest as he followed the tracks to the piñon trees, over a small embankment of rocks, down into a sandy arroyo. It was easy.

So someone other than his grandfather had actually started the fire. It hadn't been the accident of a drunken old man. But why would anyone want to harm his grandfather, Jesse wondered? He would get ahold of the police later. Clah, in particular.

Suddenly a flock of ravens rose from a treetop not far away and winged for safety. Jesse stopped dead in his tracks, searching.

Something was wrong.

Very wrong.

A familiar jolt snapped him to attention: his danger signal, a sudden, unpredictable alarm that came from inside. The last time it sounded was when he had almost stepped on a rattlesnake. He didn't know what to call it, but he knew that when the hairs on the back of his neck started to rise for no apparent reason, he'd better get ready for action.

He became aware of a thin sound, like the cry of an animal, a moment after he ceased to hear it. Then he wondered if he had heard it at all. The cry lingered in his inner ear, possibly the only place it had ever existed.

Time to turn around. Time to get out of here, his alarm told him. Beat it. Fast!

He was sure he was being watched, probably from over by the trees where the crows had fled. Who would be out there but the owner of the tracks he'd been following? The fire-starter. The skinwalker.

Although Jesse didn't consider himself superstitious, he had been raised hearing stories about witches, and it was a fact that there were those among the Diné who practiced such evil. They were to be avoided at all costs.

Jesse made an exaggerated show of carefully studying

the ground, looking this way and that for prints. He pushed the hair out of his eyes, stood up straight, and feigned bewilderment, pretending that the clues in the earth had disappeared. The cold finger touching his spine told him that the eyes were still watching him.

Trying not to seem too obvious, he shook his head in mock disappointment, then turned and headed back toward the hogan.

In the excitement of tracking, Jesse figured he must have covered about a quarter of a mile. It took all of his willpower not to turn to see if he was being followed. Taking slow, deliberate steps, he occasionally stopped to study footprints, thinking the whole time about the fire, the skinwalker, and, of course, the mysterious coins. His grandfather had said the coins had been stolen from Broken Bones, whoever that was, and then set on his doorstep by *chindi*. It made absolutely no sense.

When he was in sight of the hogan, Jesse finally turned around and surveyed the rocks and trees behind him. Nothing moved except the gentle sway of piñon branches in the mild breeze. He felt the muscles in his shoulders and the cold tightness in his chest begin to relax. But he knew he had to get his grandfather out of here. The old man's life could actually be in danger.

Chee was sitting inside the open doorway, sipping a cup of coffee, when Jesse returned. His face sagged like an aged, over-ripened melon; the whites of his eyes were glazed with specks of red and yellow. "What did you find?" he asked, his voice cracked and scratchy.

"There were some tracks leading out of here, but I

lost them," Jesse lied. No need to worry the old man even more, he figured. He pulled the cap off a plastic water jug near the door and took a long drink. The tepid water dripped down his chin, wetting his neck and chest. He took another swallow. "Come on. I think you should stay with us for awhile."

Chee grunted. "Your mother gonna protect me, or are you gonna do the job? I can take care of myself."

"I was s'posed to tell you that Mom can't take you into town until next Saturday, so you might as well come over. Besides, whoever started that fire might come back and do the same to your house. Let's go. We'll call the police from the store, then head home."

Jesse set the half-empty jug down, untied the reins to his horse, and climbed easily up on the large chestnut mare. "Come on," he coaxed. "Take my hand. I'll give you a lift. You can ride in the back seat."

His grandfather smiled and shook his head. "I'll stay. Go call the police if it makes you feel better. See if they've got any of those silver bullets for werewolves. I'm sure they'll run right over."

Jesse frowned. The chestnut pranced impatiently beneath him. He drew the reins tighter, tried to think of a way to persuade his grandfather but knew it would be an impossible task. "Mom's going to be worried about you."

"Tell her I can take care of myself," Chee snapped, his eyes resting on the Wilbur Hauck single-shot.

Jesse was sure a new cartridge was already parked comfortably inside the chamber. "I'll be back shortly," he promised, still reluctant to leave.

Chee waved a perfunctory salute and nodded. *"Hágoóneé."*

The chestnut responded gingerly to Jesse's light flick of the reins and trotted back across the patch of weeds in the direction they had come. Jesse waved good-bye, but his grandfather had already disappeared inside.

The boy rode with a relaxed and fluid motion that came from years of familiarity with horses, although at the moment he was anything but relaxed. The events of the morning troubled him. Why had someone burned down his grandfather's brush arbor? Was it some kind of warning? He questioned how the old man could have any enemies. Had his grandfather really seen a skin-walker, or had his eyes been playing tricks on him? He vividly remembered the feeling that had crept over him while he was tracking: someone or something really weird had been out there, watching. The memory kept him tense and alert as he rode down the tire-rutted trail toward the trading post. He warily searched the shadows of the trees, the jumble of sandstone formations that jutted out on either side of him. The sun was almost directly overhead and growing warmer, yet the chill of the morning's experience clung to his bones.

Most puzzling were the coins. Where had they come from? The old man's story about ghost sickness and *chindi* was confusing, but the fact remained that the coins were actually in his grandfather's possession.

Jesse opened the top button of his shirt and pulled out the leather necklace he had made. At the end of the heavy lace dangled a perforated coin, a coin exactly like his grandfather's. He held it up close, examined it for the hundredth time: three men, two of them bearded, were embossed on one side, a shield decorated with a lion was on the other. Had this one, too, been a gift from the dead?

Sunlight reflected off the tarnished portraits, causing them to shimmer. It was as if the faces were smiling at him, confident that their secret was hidden forever.

CHAPTER THREE

Carolyn Manchester stood near the large windows overlooking Gallup's tiny airstrip, her soft-leather luggage pooled around her. She balanced her weight on one foot, then the other, brushed a strand of dark brown hair away from her eyes, and watched another small plane touch down on the runway.

An observer would have immediately noticed that the tall, slender girl wearing dark-rimmed glasses was as foreign to the region as her impatience implied. In a tract of country predominantly populated by Navajos, where time was viewed as a generality, rather than a specific, the stylish, impatient young lady stood apart. An island of fashion amidst a sea of jeans, T-shirts, and cut-offs. She pulled her sleeve away from her slim wrist, exposing a lady's Rolex, and glanced at it before returning her gaze to the window.

Carolyn couldn't believe her parents had done this to her: over an hour late, and still she waited. She contemplated calling again, decided against it. Wouldn't do any good, she thought. She was sure she'd get the same response. "Red Rock Trading Post. Who? No, they're not here. They went to Gallup. Won't be back until late this afternoon. . . . This is who? Oh. Hmm. Well, I'm sure they're on their way," the woman's quiet, slightly accented voice had informed her. Such was her welcome to New Mexico, she thought. They couldn't even get here on time to greet her. Probably too caught up with selling trinkets and baubles at the stupid old trading post they had bought. That seemed to take precedence over everything else these days, especially her.

More people came through the glass doors at the entrance, some coming, others going. Her anger mounted. She had traveled across the entire continent, been on one flight after the other since early this morning, and yet her parents couldn't pull themselves away from what they were doing long enough to make it to the airport on time.

Over the intercom, a man's voice heralded the arrival of Mesa Airlines Flight 160, which was now boarding for Farmington and Durango. An elderly Indian woman accompanied a uniformed young man to the boarding gate. Probably her grandson, Carolyn guessed. The woman was dressed in voluminous layers of gathered skirts, and her white tennis shoes flashed underneath. She wore a blue velvet blouse, a turquoise necklace, and silver bracelets. Her thinning black hair was tightly scraped back, tied with white string in a heavy knot at the nape of her neck. A small but imposing figure.

The young man kissed her cheek; she took his hands in hers and spoke softly in his ear. Carolyn turned away, allowing them a moment of privacy.

She again looked at her watch as another possibility crept into her thoughts: Maybe her parents had been in an accident. Maybe they were lying in hospital beds at this very moment. Or worse yet, maybe they were trapped inside their crushed vehicle somewhere, hidden at the bottom of some dark, God-forsaken canyon. Carolyn forced the image away and concentrated on watching the entry.

Minutes dragged by. She paced to and from the pivot point of her luggage, watched the doors, the clock, the doors. Finally, she sat down and pulled out her father's letter from inside her book and reread it for the hundredth time:

May 11

Dear Carolyn,

Greetings from Mom and Dad, and Happy Birthday!

Well, we've already been down here a month; can you believe it? We've been awfully busy, to say the least. Most of the work has gone into remodeling the inside of the old trading post, and we're just now beginning to do an inventory of goods so we'll be able to begin restocking soon.

We've made a number of good friends here already, and we've decided not only to keep all the old employees but to hire a few more. As I've mentioned, the trading post is the hub of the entire area, so there's seldom a moment of inactivity. Your mother and I are sure you're going to love it out here, although it may take some time getting used to it.

I needn't tell you that the Red Rock community is a far cry from Boston. Life on the Navajo Reservation, "Diné Bakiyah," as they call it, is life without much hustle and bustle. You'll notice right away that every-thing is at a much slower pace. It's a good change for your mom and me.

The area is sparsely populated; homes are spread out miles apart, dotting an area of mostly rolling hills and mesas. It's quite beautiful. Piñon and juniper trees are abundant, and the rocks and soil have the most marvelous reddish tint to them.

One of the Navajo employees told me that after a rain the soil around here forms a type of clay that makes it nearly impossible for driving. We haven't experienced that, yet. The road from Gallup to our place is paved, but all other roads in the area are merely tire-rutted trails, often impassable after a shower. There are a num-ber of kids around your age that live nearby, so we're sure you'll make plenty of friends.

I've enclosed your itinerary along with your tickets. Your flight is scheduled for the 28th. Uncle Bob has already offered to give you a lift to the airport. Don't worry about bringing too many of your things. We already have a lot of your clothes, and whatever can't be packed in your suitcases can always be shipped to us later.

We're so excited to see you! Your flight from Albuquerque to Gallup will be on a small commuter plane, probably not much larger than the Cessna we used to have. Gallup's airport is tiny, so we'll have no trouble finding each other.

We love you. Mom says she will give you a call before you leave.

Carolyn tucked the letter back into her book and

stared out the window. She was still amazed that her parents had done this crazy thing: It was so illogical. Why New Mexico? Why a broken-down trading post out in the middle of nowhere? She could understand it somewhat if they had moved to Santa Fe, but out on an Indian reservation? What were they trying to prove? Had they been that unhappy in Boston?

Her parents had everything: a beautiful home, plenty to do, and since her father had chosen early retirement, plenty of money. They traveled. They socialized. They sent their kids to the best schools. They had the best of everything.

Up until two years ago, Carolyn's father had been co-owner of Manchester-Hawk, LTD, an exclusive chain of outdoor wear, high-tech toys, and gadgetry shops. Jack Manchester had opened the business on a wing and a prayer, as he always said, with his pal from school, David Hawkins— "Hawk," as Jack called him. That had been twenty-five years ago. And now it was all gone.

Her father's decision to sell his share of the business had come as a shock, to say the least. He had told Carolyn that he wanted more time with his family—time for travel and for experiencing new places. And travel they did. Last year her parents toured Europe, Australia, and Japan. This year, it had been an overland excursion of the United States: Daytona Beach, Mount Rushmore, Yellowstone, and, finally, the Grand Canyon.

It was during this latter trip that her parents discovered the trading post. They had come home excited; Dad said it was just the kind of business he wanted: back to basics. It would involve direct contact with customers, which was something he said he had missed with the huge establishment of Manchester-Hawk, and he loved the idea of selling everything from horse blankets to pots and pans. He said it was *his* kind of store.

And even more surprising, her mom had gone along with it. She saw the trading post as the perfect setting for her future novel, she had told Carolyn. While her father ran the store, she would be able to write.

Although Beverly Manchester wasn't a household name yet, she was working on it. She had two romance novels under her belt, both set in eighteenth-century Massachusetts: *Distant Fires* and *Salem's Thunder*. And although they weren't bestsellers, they weren't doing too badly either. Her mom felt it was time to find a new locale for her next novel, and the Southwest had been her first choice.

So here Carolyn sat: stranded in a hokey little airport, leaving almost everything that was important to her back in Boston just to spend the summer in nowhere. She was certain she'd die of boredom; there would be no shopping malls, no friends, no riding stables, no Thomas. The image of Thomas's handsome face stabbed her heart. She missed him already. Oh, she was going to have a great summer, you bet. If the school dorm would have remained open over the summer months, she would have just stayed at Regis.

She stood up again. Where were her parents? Should she try calling again?

Suddenly, there they were: Her mom and dad whisked through the all-too-familiar doors of the airport, noticed her at the exact moment she caught sight of them, and ran to embrace her.

CHAPTER FOUR

Carolyn felt a medley of emotions. Relief that her parents were safe surged through her. She was overjoyed to see them again, to be with them, to hug them. But the anger smoldered inside her, threatening to burst. So, they were just simply late. That's all. No accident. No car trouble. No reason they couldn't have been here on time.

Beverly Manchester kissed her daughter's cheek and shook her head, apologizing. "We're sorry for being late, dear. We were so anxious to get here. . ."

"It sure looks like it," Carolyn blurted. "I just can't believe you let me stand here for over an hour. I was wishing that I had a ticket to just fly back to Boston."

Her father pulled himself away from her, finally noticing his daughter's mood. His deep-set eyes took in her expression and his brow raised in amused surprise. "We can hardly blame you for being upset, Cara," he said, resorting to her pet name. "But we got here as soon as we could, considering . . ."

"Considering all that you first had to get done at your stupid old trading post," Carolyn finished for him.

"That's not fair to your father and me." Beverly Manchester's warm smile had developed frost. "We certainly hadn't planned on being late."

Her father gathered Carolyn's luggage and headed toward the exit. "We have plenty of time to talk about it, and plenty of catching up to do," he said amiably. "You hungry? We can stop and get a bite before heading home. There's a real quaint restaurant near here, decorated in Santa Fe style. I'd bet you'd enjoy it."

Carolyn's mother picked up on the cue. "Your father's right. We can discuss it later. We're sure you're exhausted after all that traveling. Tell us, how was your trip?"

The first thing Carolyn noticed as she stepped out into the New Mexico sunshine was the intensity of the sky. A brilliant blue filled its overwhelming breadth; the air was dry, the atmosphere luminous: so unlike the hazy, opaque skies over Massachusetts. She watched her dad load the luggage into the back of a Jeep Cherokee.

"What do you think of it?" he asked, slamming the rear door shut. "We traded in the Lincoln last month. It didn't seem too practical on the rez. The suspension was too low."

"That's part of it," her mom added. "It was also a bit too flashy. Your father identifies with the Jeep more than the Lincoln."

"Right. The outdoorsy type, even if I am a *bilagáana*," he grinned. When he smiled like that, even Carolyn could see the features she shared with her father: same wide mouth, same open face that expressed a gamut of feelings.

"What's a *bila-* whatever?" she asked as she slid into the back seat. She was beginning to regret her outburst a few minutes ago. Not exactly the way she'd pictured their reunion.

27

"A *bilagáana*," her father repeated. He backed the vehicle out of the parking space and headed for the airport exit. "It's Navajo for 'white person.'"

Her mother turned around to face her. "Should we stop and get something to eat? You must be famished." She was once again smiling, the incident in the airport forgotten.

Carolyn noticed her mother's dark tan, the leaner, healthier look to her face, her new short-cropped haircut. The change of climate seemed to agree with her. Even her eyes seemed brighter, more alive. "Not really," Carolyn responded. "I ate lunch in Albuquerque. I'd just as soon get home." She cringed at her use of the word "home." She couldn't really consider that her residence from now on was a trading post out on an Indian reservation.

"Fine with us," her father replied.

They passed a smattering of stores with bold signs declaring Zuni and Navajo jewelry, kachina dolls, Indian pottery. Some promised quality, others advertised low prices and cash for pawn. They turned south on Highway 602 and wound through sandstone buttes and mesas. A sprinkling of cedars dotted the terrain, adding flecks of green to an otherwise ochre landscape.

"You won't believe it," her father ventured, "but we had actually given ourselves plenty of time to get to the airport. We just hadn't anticipated the squaw dance."

"Squaw dance?" Carolyn repeated.

"It's a healing ceremony conducted by Navajos in the summer months," her mother explained. "I think they call it *Entah,* or something like that—it means

28

'Enemy Way.' It used to be given as a purification rite for warriors who'd been contaminated by being in contact with an enemy; now, I believe it's performed for persons whom the local medicine man diagnoses as sick due to contact with non-Navajos."

It all sounded so foreign to Carolyn. "What does that have to do with being late at the airport?" she asked, reluctant to believe anything but negligence was the reason for her having to wait so long.

"The squaw dance is a three-day ritual," her father said, "which begins at the patient's hogan, those octagonal log dwellings you see out there. It then moves to a new location each succeeding day, usually a day's ride on horseback."

"A ceremonial staff, decorated with feathers and long ribbons, is carried by one of the young riders, accompanied by men on horseback," her mother added. "Today they happened to take a route that paralleled the road. There must've been thirty or forty pickup trucks and cars in the caravan behind the riders. The road is very winding so, of course, it was impossible to pass."

Jack Manchester nodded. "We must have been behind them for nearly an hour, driving along at about five or ten miles an hour. Just goes to show you that Boston isn't the only place where you have to worry about traffic jams."

Carolyn realized with reluctance that she'd been unfair to her parents. She should apologize, she knew, but she couldn't muster the words. Apologizing had never been one of her strong points. She stared out the window, watched the scenery evolve from stubby trees into taller ones. They passed a sign reading "Welcome to Zuni."

"Are we almost there?"

Her father shook his head. "Nope. We're just cutting through a small slice of the Zuni rez. They're a Pueblo tribe, very different from the Navajos. The Pueblos tend to cluster close together in adobe or stone villages, like Halona Itawana, the Zuni community. It's been around since before Columbus, and it's still inhabited."

"Matter of fact," her mother added, "Halona Itawana is one of the legendary Seven Cities of Cíbola that Coronado and his conquistadors plundered. They didn't find any gold, though. The whole story about a golden city had been a monk's delusion. I intend to incorporate it into my next novel, *Gold and Glory*. I'll have to tell you about it."

Carolyn nodded.

"You see, Cara," her father explained in his Father-Is-Explaining-Something voice, "there're quite a number of Indian reservations in New Mexico. Some belong to Pueblo tribes like the Zuni and Acoma, others are home for the Navajos or Apaches.

"The Navajos, whom we have most contact with at the store, live quite differently from the Zuni. Their religion is different and so is their culture. Navajos usually live very spread out from one another. Their hogans and trailer houses make up camps of a few families, which will oftentimes be at least a quarter of a mile away from the next group. Many families raise sheep, and they need the space so they won't infringe on their neighbor's grazing land. As you noticed on our way out of Gallup, most of their homes are quite primitive according to our standards. Some families still lack electricity. Most don't have plumbing. Water has to be hauled in, often from wells that are quite a distance away. That's one reason you'll notice so many pickup trucks out here."

"Which tribe is the biggest?" Carolyn asked, finally somewhat interested.

"The Navajos, by far," her father answered. "Diné Bakiyah, as they call it, stretches across the Four Corners region of Arizona, Utah, New Mexico, and Colorado. It's roughly the size of Vermont and New Hampshire put together."

"That big?"

"Mm-hm. That's just the main reservation. There are also three other Navajo bands detached from the main rez: Ramah, where we're located, Cañoncito, and Alamo. In addition, there's the so-called 'checkerboard' area that is made up of countless patches of land added and subtracted by the federal government over the past ninety years. It's a lot of country, especially considering that the total population is under two hundred thousand, less than half the size of Plymouth County in Massachusetts."

"It's a lot of open country," Carolyn's mother added. "And we love it."

Carolyn again nodded but said nothing. A lot of open country, she mused, wondering how she would kill time during the long stretches of summer. No malls. No tennis. Worst of all, no riding.

Her mother seemed to read her thoughts. "How's your riding coming along? Tell me about the *Prix Caprilli.*"

"We did really great." Carolyn perked up. "We came in first in all categories. Miss Hamershein said we had the highest score of all the riding clubs."

"Fantastic," her father interjected. "Wish we could've been there to see it. Who were you riding?"

"Pensive Motion. She's the same thoroughbred I rode at Worcester last spring, remember?"

"Mm-hm. She's a great horse. Very intelligent."

Her mother turned around in her seat to face her. "We know you've made some sacrifices to come stay with us this summer, Cara. We appreciate that. And although there may not be riding clubs out here, we might be able to work something out so you can still be riding."

Carolyn just stared out her window. There was no way her riding could be replaced. Surely she would suffer next fall from her lack of practice during the summer.

Ever since she had been seven years old, Carolyn had taken riding lessons at Winston Heath Livery Yard. Then after three years of lessons, she had ridden in dressage competitions for the past four years, and she was planning on beginning practice for show jumping this summer. Well, kiss that dream good-bye.

She had an inborn love for horses. Her instructor, Miss Hamershein, had praised her as one of the finest young talents she'd ever coached.

Carolyn had already competed in countless dressage competitions, and last month's *Prix Caprilli* was the year's main event. The test was ridden from memory, and emphasis was placed on the rider's ability, coordination, control, and style. It included two small fences, approximately two feet in height, that were jumped from a trot and canter. Emphasis here was placed on fluidity and well-balanced movement. Judges graded on the performance of the horse, its elegance and presence, and the ability of its rider. Carolyn had practiced more than a hundred hours, and it had paid off. Miss Hamershein said she was already earning a reputation among the riding clubs as someone to keep an eye on in the years ahead. Well, her competitors were certain to benefit from her summer wasted in New Mexico. They would be practicing all summer while she stocked shelves at an old trading post.

Her father turned left at the junction for Highway 53. After they passed through the small hamlet of Ramah, the landscape once again turned into high desert and vast canyons. They turned right off 53 and traveled over a narrow, pitted road that deteriorated with every mile. The Jeep bumped along through some of the most beautiful country Carolyn had ever seen.

Sandstone monoliths jutted dramatically out of the red earth. Some looked like petrified dinosaurs, others took on human shapes, like trolls long ago turned into stone. Deep green piñons and juniper contrasted sharply against white sandstone crags. Long-bladed yucca were everywhere, their center stems still in blossom, standing straight and proud. Wildflowers dotted the cheat grass, sprinkling a mixture of colors across the countryside. Purple-shadowed mesas stood majestically ahead of them.

Climbing the winding road to the very base of a butte, they finally arrived at Red Rock Trading Post— *home,* as Carolyn's parents now called it. The Jeep came to a dusty stop in the now-deserted and unpaved parking lot.

Carolyn climbed out of the vehicle and stretched; it had been a long day. She looked about with mild amusement. If she hadn't known better, she might have been able to convince herself that this was really a dream, sort of a surreal step into *The Twilight Zone*. This wasn't the twentieth century—it was someplace in a time entirely of its own.

CHAPTER FIVE

The tilted sign on the door read "Sorry. We're Closed." Apparently, the action at Red Rock Trading Post came to a sudden halt after six P.M. Several stray dogs, thin and rough-coated, ignored the message and waited patiently for a handout. Their attentive eyes watched the family's every move.

Two rusted gas pumps, antiques by the look of them, stood sentinel in front of the old store. The rough stone building looked like a relic out of the Wild, Wild West, belonging in an old photograph, not in Carolyn's summer. An ancient soft-drink sign hung askew from a low-set eave; another sign declaring "Feed Sold Here" leaned against the wall. Surplus tires lay atop the low-pitched, tin roof, obviously to hold everything in place during winds.

"We've mostly been concentrating on remodeling the inside up to this point," her father commented, somewhat defensively.

"Oh," Carolyn managed.

"Would you like a tour? The employees have all left for the day, but I'd be glad to show you around."

"Not now, dear," Carolyn's mother said, coming to her rescue. "Give her a chance to unpack and freshen up. Let's show her the cottage."

Carolyn was led around back, still in a daze, wondering if maybe she were dreaming. The "cottage" was a tiny stone house constructed in a checkerboard pattern of brown and red sandstone blocks, with a roof of stripped logs. A light breeze rustled, moving cheerful sun dapples back and forth against the building. Nearby, a large cottonwood shaded the thin patches of grass struggling to survive; Carolyn assumed this would be considered the yard. She reflected back on the beautiful two-story red brick home they had once owned, the gently rolling sea of Kentucky bluegrass that had once been her back yard, the neatly sculpted islands of flowers and shrubs. She willed herself out of the memory, shuddered inwardly, and smiled. "It's nice," she said.

Directly behind their home rose a sandstone butte, at least two hundred feet of sheer, smooth, red stone, laced with blow holes and caves. Strange-sounding birds cawed overhead, circling in lazy motion against the pale sky.

"Come in, Cara," she heard her mother say. "Let me show you your room. I'm afraid it's a bit small compared to our old home, but I'm sure you'll find it comfy."

Comfy indeed, Carolyn thought. After passing a tiny kitchen area, a gloomy and cramped living room, and a claustrophobic hallway, here it was: the comfy bedroom. No room for a desk or a double bed, for that matter. Just a comfy single-width cot. Next to the cot stood a small, forlorn-looking nightstand, dwarfed by a lamp that she recognized from her old bedroom. It looked so out of place in this new setting that Carolyn couldn't help but laugh. And once she started laughing, she couldn't stop. She dropped her carry-on bag, flopped onto her cot, and exploded. She laughed so hard she was crying. Her mother and father squeezed into the room and stared at her, puzzled smiles on their faces as they tried to comprehend what was so funny. Carolyn tried to control herself, but every time she looked at them, another fit of laughter erupted. She couldn't take it. Her stomach actually hurt. Stop looking at me, she wanted to cry out, but she couldn't.

Finally the attack passed. She lay there blurry eyed, smiling back at the silly, wonderful faces of her mom and dad.

"Well, are you going to let us in on what's so darn funny?" her mother asked, good-naturedly.

Rubbing her temples, she touched the bridge of her glasses with one finger, pushing them up on her nose. "No, but I sure love you both. I'm so glad to be with you. I missed you."

Her mom's eyes brimmed with tears as she sat down next to her. The cot creaked some more, sinking deeper. They hugged.

"Let me get the rest of your stuff," her father offered. "And Cara . . . we're thrilled to have you here."

Her mother stood up, still holding her hand. "Come on, let's get you unpacked. You'll notice that most of your clothes are already here."

Carolyn shuffled through the closet. Sure enough, most of her summer clothing was crammed into the tiny space. Even her riding clothes were here: her high black boots, the white jodhpurs, her hacking jacket, even her black velvet cap and white stock tie; all hung neatly, ready for use. She sighed, then began unpacking, wondering where everything was going to fit.

An hour later, she was given the grand tour of the place. It started at the cottage, which didn't take long, then moved on to the trading post. As they walked over to the store, Carolyn caught a glimpse of the sun as it sank behind the great butte. For some reason, she shivered; a premonition of danger, too subtle to surface in her consciousness, moved through her.

Her father jiggled a key in the lock, pushed against the heavy wooden door until it clicked, then pulled it open wide. A cow bell clanged overhead. Carolyn stepped into the gloomy building, secretly hoping the tour wasn't going to take long. She was starting to get hungry.

"And here's your father's pride and joy," her mother announced, flicking on the light switch.

Large, round spotlights hung from the rafters, illuminating the store with a rich golden glow. Carolyn sucked in a short breath, taken aback. It was gorgeous. Great handwoven Indian rugs hung from the upper regions of the walls, interspersed with antique rifles, Indian lances, rustic lanterns, and huge earthen pots cradled in fish netting. Below were shelves upon shelves of hardware items, clothing, groceries, and just about anything else one could need. Wooden kachina dolls cluttered several display cases, along with silver and turquoise jewelry, beaded works, and handcrafted rattles and wood carvings. Sculptures of eagles and cloaked figures stood proud and elegant on heavy stone bases, strategically positioned in the crowded store. Great oak counters, polished to perfection, ran the width of the far wall, separating an aisle where the employees would be stationed; three huge bronze cash registers were mounted on top of it at intervals of about twenty feet. Looking around her, Carolyn felt as though she were standing in a small museum rather than a general store.

Her father's face beamed with pride. "Well, what do you think? Take a look at this floor. Solid oak."

"With about a dozen coats of shellac," her mother chimed in. "The store is registered with the Navajo tribe as an historical landmark. It was built over a hundred years ago. We've tried to restore it as close as possible to its original state, and all we've had to work with are some old photographs the previous owners left us."

"Of course, we've added some embellishments of our own," her father said. "The cash registers were imported from Italy. Some of the Indian artifacts, like the lances up there, are actually replicas from the Sioux tribes up in South Dakota. The pottery is from the area, though. We have ancient Anasazi vases, modern Navajo pots, as well as Pueblo. The Acoma pottery in particular is very popular back East; I'm in the middle of setting up some marketing with dealers in New York and Toronto."

"Leave it to your father to turn a dilapidated trading post into a lucrative business. If anyone can do it, he will."

Her father smiled. "We'll see. You should've seen this place a few months ago; it was a wreck. We weren't able to open for business until about three weeks ago. Before that, your mom and I and several employees worked ten to twelve hours a day remodeling. I've sunk a lot of money into it so far, hoping it eventually pays off."

"It will," her mother assured him.

"Your mother hasn't been able to get much writing in so far; she's been giving about every minute to this place. But now that the interior is about where we want it, Spencer and I can begin work on the outside while the ladies run the cash registers, and your mother can begin work on her book."

"Who's Spencer?"

"Spencer Tsosie," her mother said. "One of our employees. You'll meet him along with the others tomorrow."

"They're a good bunch," her father added. "You'll like them."

Carolyn wandered down the aisles, examining merchandise, looking up at the beautiful Navajo rugs. She remembered seeing some in one of the small stores at the Albuquerque airport, and she had been surprised at how expensive they were. The ones in her father's store were at least twice their size.

"There's one more thing we wanted to show you, Cara, before it gets dark. Come on. We'll have to head over to the lot out back."

"I don't know about you two, but I'm getting hungry," her mother added. "Let's go quickly so I can get started on supper."

"I'll help, Mom."

"We'll see. You may not feel like it after you see what we have for you."

She looked at her mother questioningly. "See what?"

Beverly Manchester smiled mysteriously. "Come on."

After locking up, they walked single file around the cottage toward a weathered building that was either a storage shed or a stable.

It was enclosed by a wooden-railed fence that butted up against a portion of the great cliff wall.

What caught Carolyn's eye, however, was not the fence but the magnificent black horse watching them approach. He was like a statue, arrogant and proud. His delicate head was set atop a high arched neck, and not a sculptor living could have done justice to the suppleness of line on his perfectly modeled body.

"He's yours," her father said. "Happy birthday."

"W . . . what?" Carolyn stammered.

"We bought him for you, dear," her mother added excitedly. "Since we weren't able to be with you on your birthday, we decided to celebrate when you arrived. Your father searched all over the Southwest to find a horse that would suit you, and here he is."

"His name is Nakai. It's a Navajo word meaning black."

Carolyn threw her arms around her father, her eyes filling with tears. She kissed him, then kissed her mother, then her father again. She couldn't believe it: her very own horse. And such a beautiful one. "Thank you so much! I . . . I'm in shock!"

Her father draped an arm around her shoulder. "Come on, let's have a closer look at him. He's a mustang, of course, a gelding. He's barely broken. You'll have a lot of training to do. I've been told there are several Navajos around here who are pretty good with horses, and I could probably get one of them to give you a hand. But it won't be in the style of your riding school—the show riding out here is strictly rodeo type."

Her mother opened the gate, and they stepped inside.

"I bought him from a Navajo horse breeder over in Kaibeto, up in the northwestern corner of the Big Reservation," her father continued. "He's about a year and a half old. He's been ridden, but not a lot."

"Nakai," Carolyn called softly, enjoying the sound of his name.

Nakai's large eyes were watching her, his ears cupped to the sound of her voice. He suddenly jerked his head upward.

Carolyn's parents stopped midway and allowed their daughter to approach her horse alone. It was time for them to get acquainted.

"Nakai, Nakai," Carolyn kept repeating as she slowly approached the beautiful animal. The horse was tense; his nostrils quivered and he stood stock-still She couldn't believe this great, half-wild beast was really hers. *Hers.* She reached out to him, and Nakai didn't move away from her touch. He neighed, then stomped the ground nervously with a powerful front hoof.

"Nothing to be afraid of, fella."

Her hand went to his muscular neck as he side-stepped a few steps. She spoke to him again, and although his ears swept back, some of the restlessness seemed to leave his body at the soothing sound of her voice. She began leading him around the grounds by his halter, and the horse walked nimbly at her side. It was a promising beginning.

Her parents watched as she walked the gelding around the enclosure, and when they saw she meant to stay with him for awhile, they turned to go back toward the house. Quietly, they closed the gate and left their daughter with her horse.

Later that evening, after supper and birthday cake, Carolyn stayed up and talked with her parents until almost midnight. They had a lot of catching up to do. She shared some of her school experiences, briefly touching on the subject of Thomas, whom her parents had met last Christmas, then talked about her other friends, riding school, and her plans for next fall. Her mother told her about the new novel she was starting, and her father bragged about his employees. He dominated the conversation with the history of the trading post, only occasionally asking about someone back in Boston: Uncle Bob, his wife Trudy, or friends. Carolyn asked about her brother, Steve, and was told about his latest adventures at Harvard. He was continuing his law courses during summer but promised that he would try to make it out for a visit sometime in July, during break.

Carolyn yawned and curled up on the couch, trying to stay awake.

"Time to hit the sack, Cara," her father commented. "There'll be plenty of time for us to talk later. You look beat."

"There are towels in the closet next to the bathroom.

Your father and I will tiptoe around in the morning so you'll be able to sleep late."

Too tired to even comment, Carolyn kissed them both good night, thanked them again for the wonderful birthday gift, then went to her room, not even stopping to brush her teeth. She pulled off her blouse, climbed out of her skirt almost in one motion, and slipped in between the cot's cool sheets.

In a moment she was asleep, a sound sleep that would soon shatter.

CHAPTER SIX

Moonbeams washed across the nightscape, dimly illuminating the twisted stone where the wolf made his lair. As a shadow among shadows, the creature moved with quick and sinuous determination. He kicked sand upon the remaining coals of the fire, smothering its final wisp of breath. He had seen enough. It was time to look more closely.

He crept stealthily between greasewood and sage, silent as a specter. Darkness was his cloak, his mask. He moved with swiftness, each step light, precise, leaving only the slightest imprint in the sand.

Yet his thoughts were heavy.

There was still only one vision, but it had changed. It was now marked with two faces, opposites. The familiar features of old had manifested everything he'd ever desired, as he had always seen it and knew it should be. But the latest vision disclosed his destruction.

A vision with two faces, with two possibilities. This he understood. But it had never been this way before. Why the change? As often as he had looked into the flames through the prisms of his crystal, he'd never seen the other face. Until now. A change brought about by change. And the only change he was aware of was the arrival of the new owners of the trading post, the *bilagáanas* who had come from the East.

He was now warned of the danger, but the vision was as unclear as murky waters. For within the fire, reflecting past the crystalline stone, the wolf had seen his nemesis: the enemy who could expose him, the one who had the power to destroy him. The apparition had been masked in allegory, in the image of Twilight Boy, the mythological messenger-child of the Yellow Wind.

Long ago, First Man and First Woman set out to build the four sacred mountains of Diné Bakiyah. They made the mountains of earth: *Sisnaajini* in the east, *Tsoodzil* in the south, *Dibenitsaa* in the north, and *Dook'o'oosliid* in the west.

As the winds were stationed at the horizon to guard the land, First Man and First Woman ran a bolt of lightning through the mountain in the east, fastening it to the earth. They decorated it with white shells and white lightning and set Crystal Boy to dwell there as a messenger between the winds and the Calling Gods.

Then First Man and First Woman fastened the mountain in the west to the earth with a sunbeam and adorned it with haliotis shell and black clouds. They placed Twilight Boy there as a messenger between the winds and the Calling Gods.

Crystal Boy and Twilight Boy were the winds' children. Whatever messages they whispered into the ears of the Calling Gods, whatever they spoke, it would come to be.

And now he had to find this Twilight Boy. He must find him and destroy him. It troubled the wolf that his enemy had only been revealed to him as an allegorical figure, a symbol from an ancient story. What did it mean? Would he know his adversary when he saw him? And what was the significance of his enemy being portrayed as the messenger of the gods? Was there something he was overlooking? When he found this Twilight Boy, he would crush him, and the secret would remain, the power would be his.

After all these years of careful planning, he was getting so close; yet now stood the greatest chance of making errors. Caution was essential.

Beneath the cold light of the stars, the wolf glided across the open space behind the trading post. He slipped soundlessly across the landscape, staying close to the cliff wall for cover. His movements blended with the darkness, transforming his shape into the likeness of the silhouetted landscape.

A single light shone like a lonesome beacon at the front of the store. Nothing stirred. He advanced toward the cottage with utmost care, aware that he was now finally visible to anyone who might be watching.

A shrill cry suddenly split the night. The wolf froze in his tracks, willing himself to become invisible. A horse, black as the dark-wind spirit, reared in its enclosure. In a frenzy, the spooked animal leaped effortlessly over the fence and disappeared into the night. The wolf waited until the hoofbeats faded, trying to calm the hammering in his chest. Minutes passed. He crept closer.

He circled the house, peered into darkened windows, seeing only his own reflection against the curtained glass. Quietly, he tried the back door. Locked.

But a window was propped open and the curtains were parted to let in the cool night air.

He approached; his breath quickened to a pant.

Inside, illuminated only by starlight, lay a *bilagáana* deep in slumber. Her skin was as pale as white shell, her thick dark hair was matted in a tangle of curls around her face. She appeared nymphlike: her lips parted slightly, eyelids twitching, then relaxing.

The wolf's eyes narrowed to glaring slits, his jaw tightened. He willed himself into smoke, became ethereal, and entered the girl's dream world, searching . . . searching . . . for a sign of something that connected her to his vision. He tasted the slight saltiness of her skin, smelled her scent. He willed his presence to climb inside her . . . gently prying her open, forcing himself into her parted consciousness.

Carolyn twisted the covers into a ball as her sleep tormented her. The tendrils of dreams stretched to a taut fiber, then suddenly snapped. Something was wrong.

The sense of being violated forced her eyelids to flutter open. An animal with a skull-like face peered in at her from the other side of the window, then moved back just enough to transform itself into the face of a man. Carolyn's heartbeat kicked up a notch and her breathing became agitated. A dream, *something* told her.

Yet a lancet of fear slid into her belly, and she almost wet the bed. She swam up into consciousness with a scream in her throat like fire, but still she was mute. The face beneath the animal skull was still there, staring at her with an evil intensity. Carolyn blinked, thinking in a way that was not quite verbal that she was

48

not in her real life but in some terrible dreamlike state from which she still hadn't wakened.

Her heart flitted in her chest like a bird, crashing against the cage of her ribs. She pushed herself upright and stared back at the creature, terror-stricken. Only then did the man-beast silently move away from the window, slowly fading into nocturnal shadows.

The scream locked inside of her suddenly surfaced. Carolyn threw her hands over her face to shut out the terrible image, but somehow she knew it was imprinted on the deepest recesses of her being.

CHAPTER SEVEN

The solid clank of metal against metal, mallet to chisel, echoed throughout the morning quiet. Holding the chisel at an angle, Jesse drove the point into the sandstone with four steady blows, causing a chunk the size of his fist to break away. It landed in the dry streambed. He dropped his tools and pulled the plastic safety goggles away from his face, allowing them to dangle around his neck from the elastic band. With fingerless leather gloves he picked up the rock and examined it, tossed it gently aside, then studied the waist-high parent rock, his fingers exploring every detail of its surface.

It looked good. The fresh fracture was bright and clean, and even the blows against it had sounded clear. The boulder had the *alive* quality necessary for sculpture. Its quartz grains were hard and consistent, which would allow the rock to be carved without too much difficulty. It would do just fine.

Scooping up his tools—two chisels, a short-handled mallet, and a bush hammer—Jesse hiked back down the shallow arroyo to where he had tethered his horse. He would come back later with the pickup and winch and haul the rock home. The installation of the winch had been his father's handiwork. There were always reminders, the subtle pulls on his heart that never went away. Now, after a year's time, they came less often, but the pain was just as sharp.

Jesse was aware of birds twittering in the trees as he climbed the sandy incline and approached his horse. A lone hawk circled overhead in the bright morning sky. A light breeze dried the sweat on his face and he was thinking of the canteen in Smiley's saddlebags when he spotted the large black horse standing near his chestnut.

Jesse stopped, barely able to believe his eyes. The mustang, alert and skittish, snorted. Smiley had backed away, stretching the rope leading to her halter to a taut band as she watched the black nervously. Jesse forced himself to relax, knowing the mustang would be able to sense his tension.

The black horse was magnificent. Tossing his head from side to side, his mane moved through the air like wisps of smoke. His coat shone blue in the sunlight and his body was strong yet graceful. Jesse noticed that he was wearing a halter, which meant that he had an owner somewhere.

They looked at each other for a long moment before Jesse slowly raised an outstretched palm and began making soft, clucking sounds. The horse stopped shaking his head and, his ears pricked forward, began to listen to him. Jesse took a step forward.

"Hágo, shi kís." Come here, my friend.

Although the mustang stood motionless, every muscle in his body was tense, ready to burst into movement.

"Hágo," Jesse implored. *"Nikis nishklíh."* I am your friend.

He inched forward, still holding out his hand, wishing all the while he'd brought some sugar cubes. The horse watched him nervously, but didn't back away. A good sign.

"Can we be friends?" Jesse spoke in English this time—perhaps this horse belonged to a *bilagáana*. Still the mustang didn't move.

"Nineh zhoni."

Jesse actually touched the horse's mane. His head jerked back, then came forward again, his flared nostrils touching Jesse's fingers.

"Good boy. That's right. See . . . I won't hurt you."

After a few minutes, Jesse felt sure he had gained the mustang's acceptance. He had always gotten along well with animals, especially horses. The trick was to stay relaxed, patiently allowing them to trust in you in their own time, their own way. He didn't know how long he stood there, but he let the gelding sniff his fingers, nibble at his flattened out palm. Finally, he dropped his head to Jesse's feet and began grazing on the few strands of cheat grass that poked through the sand.

"I'll bet you're hungry, huh, boy?" Jesse rubbed his hand along the horse's shoulder. At that moment, Jesse made up his mind: He would take the animal home. He casually walked over to his own horse, softly unsnapped the saddlebags, and withdrew a canteen. The mustang raised his head again, intently watching Jesse's every move.

Jesse unscrewed the cap and took a long drink, allowing the tepid water to drip down his chin and onto his neck. He then poured a small amount into his cupped palm and let his chestnut drink it out of his hand. He poured out more and watched as the mustang moved closer. His own horse pulled away. Jesse untied the rope around her halter and let her distance herself.

The mustang snorted and shook his head, all the while gazing at the canteen. Jesse poured more water into his hand and held it out to him.

"Want some, friend? Here . . . drink."

The black stomped nervously.

"Come here, boy. *Hágo.*"

To his dismay, the horse spun around and trotted a few yards away, then turned and watched him. His long tail swatted the air defiantly, his head wagged up and down.

"What's the matter, fella, don't you trust me?" Jesse continued to stand there, letting the water seep through the cracks between his fingers and drip onto the sand.

The black steed whinnied softly, then edged cautiously nearer. Jesse felt certain he had him now. He poured more water into his palm and waited until the horse finally decided to lap at his fingers. He tipped the canteen again, pouring a slow, steady stream over the horse's nose, letting it trickle down his tapered snout; the black sucked it up greedily.

Jesse slowly replaced the cap on the canteen and slid its strap over his head and shoulder. With the horse's mane webbed between his fingers, Jesse moved nearer to his muscular neck and spoke softly into his ear.

"We're going for a ride, boy. You going to let me ride you?"

The horse sidestepped, his ears turned back.

"Don't be afraid. *Nikis nishklíh.*"

Positioning himself near the mustang's shoulder, Jesse quickly hoisted himself onto the horse while gripping the thick mane. The horse immediately pirouetted in a tight circle, half prancing, half kicking. The horse had been ridden before, Jesse figured, or he would've been thrown already. Again, the black tossed his head from side to side, as if trying to shake off a bothersome insect. Jesse clung to the mustang's neck, keeping his eyes focused on the horse rather than on the ground, which began to spin and gyrate. His head was beginning to feel dizzy, and his stomach was caught somewhere in his throat.

Suddenly, they stopped. For one uncertain moment the horse froze. It was like being suspended in time, like being cast into the eye of a storm. Jesse knew that the worst was yet to come. He used the next few seconds to regain his balance and think fleetingly of jumping off. He could ride his mare home, let the black devil go. But as soon as the thought surfaced, it was already too late. Up the mustang rose on his hind legs, his front hooves kicking at the sky. His shrill cry pierced the morning and echoed in Jesse's head a hundredfold. Down the hooves came, then up again to the heavens.

The sun bounced up and down like a rubber ball. Jesse was lost in a tangle of horsehair and movement; his lips tingled and his fingers were numb. The danger of falling off and being trampled became very real at that moment. Fusing himself with the horse, his first and foremost instinct was to stay alive.

As suddenly as it had started, it was over. The mustang once again planted all four hooves firmly on the ground, snorted, kicked at a clump of grass, then stood as still as a statue.

Jesse stretched motionless along the horse's neck, hoping that the lights in front of his eyes would go away. Realizing he was still holding his breath, Jesse released the thick wedge from his lungs and sucked in a gasp of air. The horse, too, breathed heavily, and sweat glistened on his silky coat.

"I'm still with you, boy."

The horse pranced a few steps, still shaking his head, as he trotted across an open meadow. Jesse made no effort to restrain him. Looking over his shoulder, he was glad to see Smiley following. The gelding broke into a canter, and he crouched lower, watching the ground beneath him roll away with increasing speed. Soon they were galloping past a great outcrop of rock, flying like a windstorm across the hill. Tears welled in his eyes from the sharpness of the wind and left wet tracks on his cheeks. He clung to the horse's neck, holding onto the mane for survival.

The heart-pounding race across the countryside took them into a terrain littered with rocks that protruded from the earth like shattered teeth. The horse seemed to realize he wouldn't be losing his rider, and he finally slowed his gait. Smiley was now nowhere in sight, and Jesse could only hope that she had made her way home.

He had to get this black devil to his house somehow—either that or jump off and walk. Jesse stretched out and grabbed hold of the horse's halter. He was precariously high on the steed's neck, but he now had the leverage he needed to control the animal's head.

With the first pull to the left, the horse began his circling act again. Jesse pulled to the right. He tried to yank free, but Jesse kept pulling. The mustang shook his head up and down but finally followed Jesse's lead, straightening, and gradually allowed his rider more control. Jesse learned if he pulled subtly to either side, the horse was more apt to yield; the sharper pulls created resistance. After several more practice turns, the animal seemed ready to cooperate. It was time to head home.

The sun was directly overhead by the time Jesse and the tired mustang trotted to an empty pen behind the single-wide trailer. Home at last. The Ford pickup and the old Pontiac were both parked out front, Jesse noted, which meant his mother was home. He was relieved to find the chestnut nosing up against a bucket of oats that he had tied to the corral fence earlier that morning.

Surprisingly, the black headed into the pen without a fuss, stepped quickly over to the water trough, and dipped his nose into the shallow water. When Jesse slid off, he discovered that his legs felt like rubber. His mouth was as dry as a dustbowl. Closing and tying the gate behind him, he hobbled over to the house to let his mother know he was home.

The trailer was locked but the key was stashed beneath the bottom step of the rickety wooden porch. Jesse pulled open the thin aluminum door, went inside, and found a note lying on the kitchen table, a ten-dollar bill, and keys to the truck.

Jesse,
I got a lift to work with Lena. Stop
by store and pick up a bale of hay—
take grandpa with you. He needs to
get some groceries. Get gas.
                              Love, Mom

After stuffing the ten into his back pocket, he sat down and read his mother's note again, simply because he was too tired to get up and do anything else. He glanced at his watch: almost noon. He had to tend the horses, he knew, but his legs ached and his stomach was still unsteady.

He was surprised his mother had gone to work; Saturday was supposed to be her day off. Lena Tsosie must've come by begging her—someone couldn't make it, and they'd be short of help at the store. His mom would fall for it. She enjoyed her job; working at the trading post broke up the loneliness and monotony of being home, especially now that Jesse's dad wasn't around anymore. And they certainly needed the money.

The small pension that began at his father's death barely covered the basics. Jesse received a Social Security check, but his mother was determined to save that money for the day when he needed it for college.

Peering out the window, Jesse watched the mustang nuzzle the bucket of oats. Smiley had yielded her claim and watched the black from a safe distance. Jesse wondered who the horse belonged to and how it had broken loose. He would have to contact one of the tribal rangers and have them track down the owners, who would surely be looking for such a magnificent animal. He'd call Jimmy Bigman, a ranger friend of his father's. Jimmy would know what to do. Maybe there would even be a reward.

With a tinge of guilt Jesse reminded himself that Smiley was still saddled and the sun was getting hot enough to make a shadow sweat. He dragged himself out of the chair to tend the tired animals.

PART II
Blue/Day

CHAPTER EIGHT

The pickup bumped along the potmarked gravel road toward the turnoff leading to his grandfather's hogan. Jesse thumped the clutch and shifted the battered Ford into third gear, all the while twisting the knob on the truck's radio. A speaker inside the sun-faded dashboard sputtered and hissed as he tried to tune in KTLN out of Window Rock. No luck. He peered into his side-view mirror, watched the dust behind him drift upward. Hot air blasted through the open window, swatting his shirt sleeve and just barely reducing the temperature in the cab.

Nearing a bend in the road, Jesse pumped the brake, punched the gearstick into neutral, and turned onto a tire-rutted trail that headed south. Parallel tire tracks tilted at a sharp slant. He wrestled the Ford into low gear and followed the trail at a precarious angle. Tall weeds between the tire ruts slapped the belly of the vehicle as it lumbered down a steep incline lined with boulders and prickly pear cactus. The truck tilted in the opposite direction as soon as it began the ascent over a small bluff. White-winged butterflies scattered in a blur of motion.

Atop the knoll, Jesse could make out the hogan about a mile farther down the sloping, winding trail. It blended in with the knots of piñon and juniper.

Inside Jesse's shirt, something touched his skin: the gold coin. It suddenly felt larger and heavier than it had before. He clutched it through the thin cotton fabric, wondering if his grandfather had had any more unwelcome visitors. His earlier experience of feeling watched from the trees caused an involuntary shiver. He probably should've shown his grandfather his coin and added another piece to the mysterious puzzle, but as he thought about it he knew that it would have added more confusion for the old man.

If his grandfather had only explained things more clearly, Jesse was sure that he could figure it all out. But the old man had been so secretive. What had he meant by saying he had *stolen the coins from Broken Bones?* And that he had returned them to *the land of the dead?*

His grandfather was getting pretty old, maybe getting senile or something. Maybe it was his drinking.

The coins bothered Jesse. Especially *his* coin. Not only was it an exact replica of the ones his grandfather claimed were left at his doorstep by *chindi,* it was also one of the few things retrieved from his father's wrecked vehicle on the night of his death.

Jesse remembered stepping out of the police station that morning, the day before his father's funeral. Roland Clah, his father's partner, had handed him his father's wallet, which carried the bronze star emblazoned with the inscription "Navajo Police." It rested atop the soft leather holster of his father's Colt. Along with the badge and pistol, Officer Clah had handed him the strange coin.

"This was in your dad's pocket," he had said, digging into his own pants pocket. "Must've been his good luck charm or something."

Jesse had never seen it before.

"It's a beauty," Clah added. "Maybe you could have it fastened onto a key chain, you know . . . make it into a keepsake." His eyes dropped to the floor. After an awkward pause, he looked directly at Jesse. "I'm really sorry about your dad, son. He was a good friend, and a good cop."

Jesse had mumbled something that sounded like thanks. His mother seemed totally unconscious of Clah; she stood by the door and stared out the window. Large dark glasses covered much of her small face, yet it was easy to read her feelings. He remembered guiding her down the steps toward Uncle Alex's pickup, helping her in, and then the weary ride home. His mother stared down at the wallet and pistol for most of the drive, weeping silently, then shuddering as large tears finally trailed down her cheeks behind the glasses. Uncle Alex drove back with one arm resting on his sister's shoulders, at a loss about how to comfort her.

Jesse pushed the memory aside as he pulled up to his grandfather's. The charred remains of the brush arbor looked about the same as they had a few days ago, except nothing was smoldering now. There hadn't been any attempt at cleaning up.

Jesse wheeled in front of the hogan, lightly beeped the horn, and waited. No response. Then the old man stepped out, made a fuss of locking up, and jigged over to the truck. Jesse noticed that he had dressed up for the

63

once-a-week occasion, sporting a slightly yellowed white shirt and an oversized bolo tie, faded jeans that were wrinkled but clean, boots shining like polished wood, and a high-crowned reservation Stetson. His hair was tied back haphazardly in a loose bun, wrapped in the middle with a string of dirty wool.

"*Ya ta hey!*" he greeted Jesse, pulling open the Ford's creaking passenger-side door.

"*Ya ta hey.*" It is good, Jesse replied.

His grandfather slammed the door shut with more force than was necessary and asked, "Where's your mother?"

"She went to work today. Lena picked her up."

Explanation accepted. His grandfather stared straight ahead, a slight smile on the edges of his lips. He was enjoying himself already. Jesse shoved the gearstick into first and released the clutch with only a slight bucking from the vehicle. Although he still wasn't old enough for a driver's license, he had been driving the ancient pickup for years, and he considered himself a pretty good driver.

"When would you like me to come by and help you clean up this mess?" he asked, making conversation.

His grandfather shrugged, stared straight ahead with an expression similar to that of a child heading for a candy store.

"We could do it tomorrow," Jesse offered.

His grandfather nodded.

"Did the police come by? I called them as soon as I got to the store the other day. They said they'd send somebody over." Jesse stole a glance at his grandfather while maneuvering the truck along the tilted trail.

"*Aó*. Clah. He snooped around for awhile. Didn't tell me anything I didn't already know."

"Clah came by?" He hadn't seen him since his father's funeral.

"*Aó*. Said someone started the fire. Said someone had been snooping around my hogan. Real smart police work, huh? Said he'd keep his eyes open. What's that mean, that his eyes are usually shut? I asked him that. He said, 'Yep. I only open them when I'm around ornery old men like yourself.'"

Jesse smiled. He could picture their conversation as clearly as if he'd been there. "Did you tell him about the coins?"

No reply.

Jesse turned right onto the gravel road and headed up toward the trading post. His grandfather was just about as much company as the radio.

"Did you mention anything about seeing a skin-walker?" he asked, hoping his grandfather hadn't.

"I told him the *yee naaldlooshii* disappeared right in front of me just as I was about to shoot him."

"What did Clah say?"

"*Ádin.*" Nothing.

"Has anyone bothered you since then?"

"*Ndagá.*" No.

Not wishing to spoil his grandfather's good mood, Jesse chose his words carefully for the next question. "You told me that you had returned the coins you had stolen when you were a young boy. Where did you get them?"

His grandfather peered out the side window, ignoring him. Jesse was surprised when he responded, "I already told you, from the dead."

"You said you returned them to the land of the dead. What does that mean?" Might as well push it as far as he could.

His grandfather sat twisting his hands in his lap, looking more and more uncomfortable. Jesse felt sorry for him. It was obvious that the memories were painful.

"I put the coins in *his* casket. They were sealed in with He Whom I Cannot Mention by Name. The coins journeyed with *him* to the voidless land of the dead." His grandfather recited this as if he had spoken the words a thousand times, like he had memorized it, imprinted it upon his soul. The words came out like a muttered chant. It was a little scary.

What his grandfather was telling him was that the coins had been placed inside the coffin with Chee's brother, buried with him! Impossible. Maybe he *thought* he had buried them, or maybe he *did* bury some of them, but somehow a few of the coins had been left out, were still in his possession to haunt him. But how had his own father ended up with a coin? Had his grandfather given him one? Had others found the same coins?

Jesse remembered asking his mother about the coin a few months after the funeral, the day he decided to drill a hole through it and make it into a necklace. She had shaken her head, said she'd never seen it before. She had even told Jesse that she doubted if the coin had been his father's, that Clah must have been mistaken. She didn't even remember Clah giving it to him. Of

66

course, as upset as she had been, it was no wonder she didn't recall.

Chee stared out the window looking miserable, and Jesse felt guilty for ruining his day. Enough questions. It was supposed to be the highlight of the old man's week. But he knew he had to somehow find out if anyone else knew about the coins, the obvious link between his father's death and his grandfather's sighting of a skinwalker. Of the four people that had a connection with the gold coins, two were dead: his grandfather's brother Tyrone and his own father. Was his grandfather's life now in danger? Obviously so, if the old man was telling the truth about the fire. And what about his own life—was he in danger too? Were there any other links connected to the coins besides himself, his grandfather, and the skinwalker? These were questions that he mulled over and over in his mind, moot little prickles that nagged him like a recurring itch.

"I found a horse this morning, Grandpa," Jesse said, changing the subject.

"Mm–hm."

"A big black one. He's the fastest horse I've ever ridden."

The cloud lifted from Chee's face and he looked over at his grandson with keen interest. "You have a new horse?"

"I found him. He's beautiful."

"You found him. Like you find firewood, or like you find a hair in your food? How do you *find* a horse?"

"I was rock hunting. He just appeared out of nowhere. He's incredible. I mean *fast*. I thought he was going to kill me when I mounted him."

"Is he branded?"

"I didn't see a brand. He must've broken free from somewhere. A horse like that would cost a fortune."

"You gonna keep him?"

Jesse shook his head. "I'll call the rangers today. If nobody claims him, maybe I'd be able to keep him."

His grandfather nodded.

The butte that was the landmark for the trading post loomed ahead of them. The road improved slightly, eventually evolving into corroded pavement. Jesse slowed the truck as he maneuvered around the large potholes that quickly matured into craters.

Glancing over at his grandfather again, he noticed that the old man already had his Social Security check in hand. Jesse smiled. The money must've been burning a hole in his pocket all week. He figured that only about half the check would be spent on food: the other half would go toward whiskey provided by local bootleggers. Since booze couldn't be purchased on the rez, bootleggers bought it and sold it at a high profit to people like his grandfather. As he watched his grandfather study the check, he again asked himself who would want to burn down the old man's brush arbor. What enemies could he have? And how did the gold coins fit into all this?

Chee looked up. "You need gas? I'll pay."

"Mom already gave me money."

"You fill it up. I'll pay."

Jesse nodded. He'd fill the vehicle with eight dollars worth while the old man puttered around in the store; that would leave Jesse enough for the bale of hay. Later, his grandfather would insist on paying for the gas, but

Jesse would refuse, saying he'd already filled it. Then a squabble would follow as a twenty-dollar bill was swapped back and forth. Jesse stood about a fifty-fifty chance of winning, depending on how enraged his grandfather got.

"On the way home, I'll need your help, Grandpa. I found another good sculpting rock. It's over by Burnt Cedar Wash. Mom wanted me to pick up some hay, so we'll be able to set it on that for the ride home."

"Aó."

He knew his grandfather loved helping him with his stones. He had even gone rock-hunting with him, patiently searching for just the right piece. His grandfather seemed to have an innate understanding of the sculpting process; he never once asked Jesse dumb questions like "What are you going to carve into this one?" or "Where do you get your ideas?" The old man seemed to understand that carving stone involved a continuous evolution. It was like chipping away the outer layers to free what was inside, releasing what was already there. Jesse had never discussed this with his grandfather simply because the old man already knew.

He pulled up at Red Rock Trading Post, parked in front of a gas pump, and waited for the dust to settle. Undaunted by the cloud of red dirt, his grandfather immediately climbed out of the cab. He slammed his door shut and hobbled off toward the store without a backward look.

CHAPTER NINE

Officer Raymond Nez parked the carry-all alongside the Begays' trailer house and peered out his open window at the sheep pen in back. The black horse pranced around and around the small enclosure, flicking its head this way and that, as if he knew he was being rescued.

Nez figured he'd been lucky. Within five hours after the call-in on the stolen horse, he'd already hit pay dirt. Not bad. A little detective work, a whole lot of luck, and bingo!

The morning had started off oddly. He had responded to a call from Red Rock Trading Post, where the new owner reported a stolen horse, apparently a horse worth a lot of money. It had disappeared during the night. What made the incident really bizarre was that as soon as he began asking the *bilagáanas* for a description of the animal, a story about someone sneaking around the daughter's window came out. The girl claimed she'd seen someone wearing an animal head, a dog's or wolf's, staring in at her in the middle of the night. Said she woke up and there he was. Her parents didn't know if she'd dreamt it all up or not. Her father had gone out to check for tracks around her window but didn't find any. Yet in the morning, when they discovered the horse missing, they concluded it hadn't been a dream after all: someone must have been outside her window.

The strangest part of the girl's story was that she had unknowingly described a skinwalker. An overactive imagination? Nez wondered. The *bilagáanas* had just recently moved to the rez and had most likely never heard of Navajo witches, unless they'd been reading some of those Tony Hillerman books.

After a half hour of questions and then looking around outside the girl's window without finding anything, Nez drove away, doubting that he'd ever even get a glimpse of the missing horse. There were simply too many folks who would love getting their hands on such an animal. And since it hadn't been branded, it would be impossible to track down. It was probably out of state by now, but Nez figured it wouldn't hurt to cruise around and ask some questions. He had a lot of relatives around Standing Rock whom he hadn't seen for quite awhile, so he might as well drop in on a few and see if anyone had seen or heard anything. It'd be a good time to catch up on family gossip, maybe even get a hot lunch.

Nez's first stop was at Andy and Arletta Tso's hogan, but he didn't find anybody home. Next he tried the Goatsons. No one there saw or knew anything, but they did say to stop by sometime, bring Carletta and the girls over for supper. Shima refilled his coffee mug and teased him about the extra pounds he'd gained since he'd last been by. Next he stopped at the Benallys, the Fowlers, and then the other Goatsons. Nothing.

Finally around mid-morning Louis Gorman casually told Nez that he'd seen a big horse flying like a black cyclone across the open land near White Rock that morning. Gorman said he was just coming back with a load of firewood when he saw the black horse a ways off from the road, heading east. *Aó*—the horse had a rider. Too far away to know if it was anyone he knew or not. Nez thanked him and drove on. He tried two more homes, but no one had seen anything. Nope, he'd pass on the coffee, but thanks. Then he stopped an old woman trailing along behind her herd of sheep. She had told him she'd seen a black horse and rider heading over toward Whippoorwill Springs. *Aó*—moving east.

There were only three families living out that way: the Tsosies, who were both in their seventies; Ed and Frieda Yazzie, whose two boys were in Tucson working construction; and Sadie Begay and her boy. Nez turned off onto the well-worn trail leading toward the Begays. He almost hoped his hunch wasn't right, but he knew what he'd find even before he got there.

Bingo. Case solved.

The police radio hissed and sputtered at intervals, then uttered a long, fuzzy message. Nez snatched up the receiver and said, "I'm at Franklin Begay's, near Whippoorwill Springs. I found the horse. I don't know if anybody's home or not." He glanced over at the old Pontiac. There was no sign of the pickup. The place looked pretty empty. "I'll swing back over to Red Rock Trading Post to get Manchester to give me a positive ID on the horse. We'll need a trailer over here."

The dispatcher's voice crackled through the static.

Nez ignored it, replaced the receiver, and dug through the glovebox, pulling out a small Polaroid camera. Better get a couple of photos for evidence, he figured. Then might as well knock on the door—someone could be home.

It was unfortunate it turned out to be the Begay boy. Nez had known his father pretty well. A fine cop. It looked like the boy was starting to get into trouble now that he didn't have a daddy around anymore. It was too bad.

Nez shoved open the truck door and stepped out into the sunlight; he pushed his sunglasses up on his nose, then tugged on the waist of his britches. After stretching the kinks out of his muscles, he strolled over toward the sheep pen to admire one of the finest pieces of horseflesh he'd ever seen. The boy certainly had good taste.

CHAPTER TEN

Carolyn rang up the items—canned soup, canned soup, box of rice, noodles, bread—and then deftly bagged them from heaviest to lightest. She thanked the woman and watched her exit through the front door. Nothing to it. She was pleased with herself for learning so fast, and it was actually sort of fun. The employees had praised her, letting her know they were impressed with how quickly she'd learned to work the cash register. Surely she had done this before, they said. Carolyn had laughed and assured them she hadn't.

The events of the previous night now seemed unreal as she sat behind the counter thinking about them. Already she had allowed the terror to diminish in her memory. Maybe she had dreamt seeing the man hooded in an animal's skull. Or maybe she'd been sleeping and woke up to find the horse thief watching her, a normal, run-of-the-mill horse thief, no animal skin draped over his shoulders, no skull head, no malevolent face staring in at her. Surely no one really sneaked around wearing a dead animal's skull—did they?

According to the Navajos, there were those who did. As soon as her father had mentioned the incident to Charlotte Manygoats, one of the women who worked at the store, the story had spread like a bad smell: A skin-walker had paid a visit to the Manchester girl.

Her father's employees were sympathetic. More than that, they seemed distraught. They looked at her as if her coffin were nearly nailed shut. Charlotte had told Carolyn that she was sorry she had come all the way from Boston just to end up getting witched; she shook her head sympathetically, as though there wasn't much hope left.

Lena Tsosie suggested that Carolyn see a medicine man. "He could do a sing over you. The Shield Prayer will pray the evil back to the witch," she had assured Carolyn, watching her through thick, horn-rimmed glasses, concern on her wrinkled face.

"Did the witch take anything from you?" asked another woman. "Like a strand of your hair or a piece of clothing?"

Carolyn shook her head. "I don't think so. Why?"

A pretty Navajo woman with large, melancholy eyes whisked Carolyn out of the room. "Carolyn, your father wants to see you. Now."

She led Carolyn to the back of the store, turned, and offered a smile. "Sorry. I lied."

Carolyn stared at her, frowning.

"I just wanted to get you away from the inquisition over there. They mean well, but . . ."

Carolyn understood and smiled. "I know. Thanks. I guess it's not every day that a . . . what did they call it, a skinwalker?" The woman nodded. "That a skinwalker pays a visit. I was hoping that I might've just dreamt it all up."

"You may have," the women said. "A *yee naaldlooshii* would have no reason to bother you." Carolyn wanted to find this reassuring. The woman held out her hand. "My name's Sadie."

"Carolyn. But you already know that."

The woman gave her hand the light touch that was typical of the Navajo. So unlike the handshakes back home, Carolyn thought, where a knuckle-crushing squeeze was common.

The gossip about witches and skinwalkers quieted when her father returned to the store. She wandered throughout the store for a while before returning to the cottage. She found her mom in the dining room working on her laptop computer. Across the dining table were scattered pages from her new story. Her mom smiled when she entered, but Carolyn could tell by the distant expression in her eyes that she was engrossed in another time and place. She wandered around the kitchen, opened and closed the refrigerator, finally decided she wasn't hungry. She glanced at the phone, wishing without any real hope that it would ring, that someone on the other end would tell her that they had found her horse.

The typing in the dining room stopped.

"You hungry, hon? I could make you a sandwich."

"That's okay. I was just hoping someone would call and say they found Nakai."

There was a pause in the other room, then her mother's voice again: "I'm so sorry about everything. What a horrible night for you. I'll bet you're tired. Would you like to take a nap?"

Carolyn opened and closed the kitchen cabinet, enjoying her mother's fussing over her. "I'm all right. I think I'll go help Dad. I'll let you get back to work."

The clicking of the computer keyboard started up again as her mother's voice floated out to her: "You're a trooper. Ask your father to call the police again when he gets a chance. Maybe they have some leads." She left the house and returned to the store.

And so here she was: The first day at her new home, and she was already working a cash register; the horse that she had owned for a full six or seven hours had been stolen; she had been spied upon in her sleep by some weirdo whom the Navajos claimed was a witch; and she was trying her best to convince her parents that she hadn't been traumatized by the whole affair. Excitement in the boonies was picking up. Suddenly she was aware of a lump in her throat. She missed her old life, her old home, her friends, her safe world at Regis, Thomas. What was she doing here? How could her parents just flip-flop into a world so foreign? How did she fit into this new life of theirs? Again, she felt the unfairness of it all.

Tonight she would tell them how she felt, how it was a big mistake for her to come out here in the first place. How she hated it already. She would tell them she wanted to go back to Boston, to her friends, her riding club, tennis, swimming. She was sure she could stay at her best friend's house: Cynthia's parents were cool that way. Or even with Uncle Bob and Aunt Trudy. She could convince them. She would convince them. She'd visit for a week or two, then head back to the real world. Carolyn could actually picture herself on her flight back home, looking ahead to a summer of familiar faces and places.

The cowbell over the front door sounded, pulling Carolyn back to the present. An old man wearing a tall black hat entered, followed a moment later by a girl. On second glance she noticed it was a boy; his long black hair was wrapped in a thick bun that hung loosely along the back of his neck. She'd seen some of the older Navajo men wearing their hair that way, but it was the first time she had noticed the traditional style on someone so young. She watched him pull out a shopping cart and disappear down one of the aisles; the old man followed.

Lena Tsosie tapped her on the shoulder. "Excuse me, dear, I need some smaller bills. Do you mind?"

Carolyn shook her head no, she didn't mind. Lena opened the cash register and began counting out one-dollar bills, replacing them with tens and twenties. "Business is slow today, but just wait till next week. The first and middle of the month are always the busiest. People from the Headstart programs and Indian Health Sevices get paid then, and the government subsidy checks are issued at that time too. It gets really busy. You'll see what I mean."

Carolyn doubted it. She would be back in Boston by then. It sounded as if Lena now considered her one of the full-time employees around here, and that was scary, like maybe she would be working here next week, and the week after that, and the weeks after that . . .

Yes. She would talk to her parents tonight.

Lena vanished, and the two customers who had entered earlier were nowhere in sight. Carolyn tinkered with a pocket calculator she found behind the counter, absently pressing buttons.

"Miss Manchester?"

She looked up.

It was Harlan Mitchell, one of the men who worked at the store. He stood beside the register, fidgeting with a faded red baseball cap that he held folded in his hands. His heavy-jawed face was a map of deep-cut lines and grooves. "If I could interrupt you for a minute . . ."

"Oh. Sure, Mr. Mitchell." Carolyn set down the calculator.

"Just call me Harlan, please." His smile didn't reach his eyes. "I, uh, couldn't help but overhear about your visitor last night."

Carolyn attempted a smile. She wished she could stop being reminded of it, but she didn't say anything.

"How frightening for a young person. I would like to give you something." He pulled out a strand of small brown beads from his breast pocket and held them out to her.

Carolyn awkwardly accepted them, unsure of what to say. She began to thank him, but he interrupted her. "No need. It's a trinket. But look closely and you'll notice that each bead is a nut, actually, a piñon nut."

She examined the beads, nodding.

"They're called ghost beads."

Carolyn's smile faded as she looked up at Harlan. Great. Just what she needed: a talisman to protect her from ghosts.

Harlan Mitchell was a big man, over six feet tall, she guessed. His long, raw-boned face was serious, his mouth thin. Judging by his choice of words, she guessed he was also well-educated.

"Many Navajos believe that the beads can ward off ghost sickness caused by evil spirits." He watched her closely. "They're supposed to protect you from, uhm . . ."

"Skinwalkers?"

"*Aó*—I'm not superstitious myself, so I couldn't guarantee their effectiveness, but I'm sure they might offer some small comfort."

Carolyn was warmed by the gesture. "Thanks. That's very nice of you."

He waved her gratitude away. "Nothing. Really. A young woman and child were selling them at a roadside stand outside of Gallup. The necklaces were so inexpensive the woman was almost giving them away. My people have been in the habit of selling out cheaply for years. I felt sorry for her and bought several strands. The others are hanging from my truck's rearview mirror as ornaments.

Carolyn unfastened the small clasp and draped the beads around her neck. Harlan Mitchell smiled, but his black eyes were flat and watchful. He pushed his hair away from his brow with the sweep of a large hand, replaced his cap, and touched the brim lightly before ambling toward the door. She thanked him again, but he walked away without looking back.

Carolyn felt she had made a friend in Harlan. A rather strange friend, she conceded, but she wasn't in any position to be too fastidious in the friend department. Feeling self-conscious about the beads as well as the whole skinwalker affair, she tucked the necklace inside her blouse, just as something caught her attention at the edge of her vision. Carolyn glanced up at Tullie, and what she saw surprised her.

Thick lips, hair clipped like someone ran a lawnmower over it, eyes as cold as a mortuary, Tullie speared her with a stare that almost stopped her heart. *My people have been in the habit of selling out cheaply for years.* Hunched over a broomstick, which he held like he was ready to strangle it, Tullie stood there, watching her. Unmoving. Sickness roiled in her stomach, and a maniacal drumbeat pounded in her skull. *Why are you staring at me like that? Go away. Leave me alone!*

Another customer entered the store, an elderly woman dressed in the traditional full skirts. When Carolyn's eyes flitted back to Tullie he was gone. As she watched the woman with the voluminous skirts pay for gasoline at another till, the boy and old man appeared with a cart full of groceries. She tried smiling as she rang up the items that they unloaded. *What's going on around here? Am I going crazy or what?* The boy said something to the old man in Navajo, and he replied.

Carolyn felt perspiration on her forehead, a clamminess on her skin. "That'll be sixty-two forty-eight," she said, folding a pair of overalls and stuffing them into a bag alongside a can of kerosene and two tins of chewing tobacco. She couldn't help glancing back again and again to where Tullie had been standing. The old man placed a crumpled piece of paper on the counter. Noticing it was a check, Carolyn turned it over and tried reading the scribbled endorsement on the back. "I'll need to see some ID, sir." He pushed the check closer to her.

"Some ID. A driver's license or something."

"Why?" the boy asked.

Her smile slipping, she attempted to explain. "Because it's a policy. In order to cash the check, I'll need to see some ID verifying who he is."

"Why not just ask him?"

Carolyn focused on the boy. She hadn't expected an argument over something so commonly accepted everywhere else but out here in the sticks. He was watching her passively. A handsome boy—generous mouth; large, expressive eyes; crow-black hair. There was something about him that suggested he was lonely, though.

"That's not the point," she replied.

"What *is* the point?"

Carolyn felt herself getting flustered. Tullie appeared again, sweeping the floor vigorously "The point is, a person who wants to cash a check has to have ID," she said, trying her best to ignore the demented broom man. "It may sound stupid and it probably *is stupid,* but so are your questions. And if you have any more stupid questions, you'd better ask someone else. I don't even work here. Okay?"

To her surprise, the boy smiled. The old man watched them stoically. He moved his hand slightly, unsure if he should retrieve his check or not.

Hearing the commotion, Lena came scurrying over. She said something to the boy in Navajo; he shrugged, said something in return.

Lena picked up the check and handed it to Carolyn. "It's okay. We'll accept it."

Feeling humiliated, Carolyn dug into the till and

pulled out bills for change. Without looking up, she asked the boy if the old man wanted large bills or smaller ones.

"Ask him. He speaks English."

With flushed cheeks she held her temper. "Sir, do you want your change in large bills or smaller ones?"

"Small," he grunted. She counted his change and handed it to him. "Thank you," she managed.

The boy spoke to Lena again in Navajo, saying something that ended in a higher tone, sounding like a question. Lena answered. The only words that Carolyn understood were "Manchester" and "Boston." The boy said something else. Lena laughed, then answered. He and the old man picked up their bags and lumbered toward the door. When they were out of ear's range, Carolyn turned to Lena. "What did he say about me?"

Lena chortled. "He asked me who you were. I told him you were the daughter of the new owner, that you just arrived from Boston."

"What else?"

"That's about it."

"He said something else, and you laughed," Carolyn persisted.

"Oh, that." She giggled. "He said you were pretty, but rude."

"Rude? How was I rude? I simply asked to see some ID before cashing a check. That's how I've always seen it done—it's just common sense."

Lena blinked. "It's different out here. Navajo manners would never permit a young person to question an elder. By asking for identification, you were inferring that you didn't trust the old man. A Navajo would never do that. An old man like Chee is addressed as *Hosteen* Chee, in respect for his years and wisdom. If he would've handed the check to another Navajo, even if the person didn't know him, he or she would never have questioned the check, even at the possibility of losing money." She shrugged. "It's just different out here."

Carolyn walked over to the door and peeked outside. Several trucks were at the gas pumps, along with an old car that had somehow escaped auto wreckage for the past twenty years. The old man was now sitting in the cab of a brown, badly used pickup truck; the boy was filling a water drum mounted in back.

When she turned around, she almost bumped into her father. He smiled at her, eyes brimming with excitement. "They think they've found him, but we need to go with the police to make a positive ID."

Carolyn looked dumbfounded. She was still thinking of the old man and his check.

"Nakai," her father said, looking at her with a puzzled expression. "I think they've found your horse. Do you want to go see?"

CHAPTER ELEVEN

Carolyn's father swung the Jeep onto an abraded trail, following Officer Nez's carry-all across a remote tract sparsely populated with juniper and greasewood. Nez's vehicle dipped, then lurched sharply to the right as it clung to the tilted twisting path that the Navajos called a road. Carolyn couldn't help but wonder what it would be like after a heavy rain. Her father slowed, carefully maneuvering over the deep ruts. Carolyn stared ahead nervously, hoping to catch sight of Nakai around each bend.

She glanced up at her father and noticed his furrowed brow and the concentration on his face. She knew he was concerned about how to handle the situation. Nez had told him that the horse had been found at the home of Sadie Begay, the woman who had befriended Carolyn only a few hours ago. The police were waiting to question her son about the theft, and even now his mother was in the truck with Nez, worried and frightened. What bothered her father, Carolyn supposed, was the fact that he might have to press charges against one of his employee's kids.

"When we get there, Cara, I want you to sit tight and let me do the talking," her father directed, apparently not trusting his daughter to keep her mouth shut.

"Why? Can't I get out and look at Nakai, make sure he's all right?"

Her dad scowled at her across the seat, then gave one of his Father-Knows-Best expressions. "I'll look him over. You stay in the Jeep." There was an edge of irritation to his voice.

"Okay."

"This is going to be a sticky matter. I don't want to hear any accusations, or any lip—I just happen to know a young lady who's rather accomplished in that department."

Carolyn ignored the remark. "Do you think they'll arrest him?"

"I don't know. Maybe. But maybe not. As you've seen, the boy's mother is quite upset already. Maybe the scare of having the police out here will be enough to straighten him out. We'll just have to see."

"And maybe he should go to jail," Carolyn persisted. "Maybe it's the kind of lesson he needs. You're forgetting he's also a Peeping Tom."

Her father nodded. "Could be. But I somehow find it hard to believe that this kid lurks around at night wearing an animal's skull, trying to cast spells on people or whatever skinwalkers are supposed to do in their spare time."

She looked over at him.

"Yeah, I've heard the rumors, too. And I've met this boy; he couldn't be much older than you. He seemed like a nice-enough kid, not someone you'd imagine wearing a wolf's head as a hat and putting hexes on people."

"Real funny."

Carolyn couldn't believe this. Her father was already sticking up for the kid. What a pushover. "I already told you I might've dreamt the part about the animal skull; I don't know. But I know that I *did* see someone looking in my window, and you know that whoever stole Nakai is also the guy who was at my window. Who knows what he was doing out there. Maybe he was just early for trick-or-treating, or maybe he was trying to rob us. Or maybe . . ."

"That's enough, Cara. Let's deal with one thing at a time. Let's get the horse back, then discuss the rest with the police. We'll take it from there, okay?"

They wound around another bend, and a home suddenly popped into view. Nez's vehicle was already parked in front of the single-wide mobile home, beside another Navajo Police carry-all. A large white truck and horse trailer were parked off to the side. From where they were, Carolyn thought she could make out Nez and Sadie standing with another police officer and a boy. She tried to make out the boy's face, but at this distance his features were invisible. The small crowd watched them approach.

A moment later, Carolyn's jaw dropped. She could see the thief clearly now and recognized him as the long-haired boy who'd been at the store earlier that morning. She pushed her glasses back up into place and gazed at the group on the small wooden porch. It was like a play in mime. Sadie Begay was shaking her head, gesturing with both hands. Nez appeared to be inspecting his boots, and the other officer was busy scribbling something into a tiny notebook. The boy stood by the open door, looking as if he planned to dodge back inside if things became too heated. He looked over at his mother sullenly, occasionally shrugging his shoulders or saying something. His whole demeanor was impassive, indifferent. So much for her father's theory of the kid being shaken up by the presence of the police.

Her father parked next to the truck and trailer, and as he backed up into the shade of the trailer, she caught a glimpse of a black horse behind the mobile home. A man was trying to lead the stallion out of a sheep pen but was having trouble; the horse jerked his head upward, attempting to rear.

"Look!" she cried. "There's Nakai."

Her father climbed out of the vehicle. "Wait here. Let me see what's going on."

As soon as he shut his door, Carolyn scrambled out of the Jeep and ran toward her horse. Her father looked over his shoulder and stopped, but she kept running, pretending not to notice. She expected to hear a reprimand at any moment, but it never came.

The man in the corral had tied a rope to Nakai's halter and had managed to lead the stallion toward the trailer. He frowned at Carolyn.

"Stay back," he barked.

"Where are you taking him?" Carolyn demanded, not intimidated in the least by the man's sharpness.

He didn't answer until the stallion was secured inside the trailer.

"Wherever I'm told," he replied. "I wouldn't open that. The horse is under police custody until an adult signs for it. Run along."

Carolyn could hear her horse snort and stomp inside the cramped trailer, but she couldn't get past this jerk to comfort him. Defeated, she watched Mr. Rudeness climb into his truck and slam the door. He started the engine, and she heard the whine of the truck's air conditioning as it kicked in. The man settled into the cab as if he expected to be there awhile. Carolyn had no choice but to leave Nakai and go back to the front of the house.

Her father was standing a respectful distance away from the porch, talking to one of the police officers. Nez and Sadie Begay were still arguing; the boy stood there too, still aloof. When he looked up, he stared at her with a very deliberate absence of expression.

Carolyn glowered at him, hoping he could read her contempt. He appeared not to notice, looked up at Nez for a moment, shrugged his shoulders again, then said a couple of words.

"I thought I told you to stay in the truck," her father scolded.

"A guy loaded Nakai into a trailer behind the house, and I had to ask him where he's taking him." It was a lame excuse at best, and she knew it.

"This is Officer Clah," her father said. "If the horse is Nakai, he wants us to follow him back to the station to fill out a statement."

"It's Nakai."

Clah spoke to her father. "Maybe you need to have a look at the horse yourself, just to confirm it."

"She knows horses better than I do. If she says it's her horse, then it's her horse."

Her father turned to face her. "Officer Clah told me that the Begay boy claims he found the horse over by White Rock early this morning. He says he rode Nakai home, then went over to the store to call the rangers. He said he couldn't get through; considering the phone service out here half the time, I could believe it."

"He's lying," Carolyn countered, once again glowering at the boy. Their eyes locked for a moment before Carolyn looked back at Clah. The police officer seemed bored with the whole affair, or maybe it was just his normal expression. She wished Nez was handling their end of things instead of Clah.

Clah was noncommittal. "I'm afraid that's something juvenile court will decide if your father wants to press charges. From my understanding, there weren't any footprints or fingerprints found at the scene to implicate the boy being anywhere near your place, nor did anyone see him steal the horse. His story is possible since a horse like that would tend to escape a corral now and then. But the decision of whether or not to file charges depends on your father." It was clear that Clah believed the boy.

"Does the boy look like the person you saw at your window last night?" her father asked. Carolyn studied him for only a second, then dropped her eyes to the ground. She shook her head no. Clah watched them, waiting for an explanation.

"My daughter awoke last night and saw someone at her window. That's why we're certain the horse was stolen and didn't simply break loose."

Clah glanced over at the boy and began to say

something, then decided against it. He was careful not to offer advice either way. "That could be added to your statement at the station, if you'd like. We'll need to see your registration papers on the horse, Mr. Manchester, as well as your permit to have livestock on the reservation. If you'd like to follow me back, we could stop by your home and get everything taken care of immediately; then you can have your horse back."

Her father nodded. "Thanks. We'll do that."

Carolyn walked back to the Jeep, lagging a few feet behind so she could turn around and shoot a final glare at the boy. He pretended not to notice.

By evening Nakai was once again in her possession, and, like the night before, she stood next to him in the stable, running her hand through the thoroughbred's long mane. "Welcome home, fella," she cooed softly.

Nakai neighed, shaking his beautiful head. He seemed glad to be back, Carolyn thought.

She took the water pail from its corner of the stall and set off for the faucet outside. The sun had just set, and the darkening sky seemed to shimmer. Returning, she set the pail near her horse. He pushed his muzzle down to the water and drank.

A few minutes later, Carolyn was at the feed box, scooping up a container of oats. While the horse ate, she cleaned the stall and pitched new straw onto the floor. Next, she took a brush and moved it over Nakai's body, brushing the dirt from his mane and shoulders. Nakai moved uneasily, but Carolyn continued talking to him. When she finally left her horse's side, the stars were bright overhead.

CHAPTER TWELVE

In Carolyn's dream, a hideous monster, part man and part dog, searched for her in the dark. Finding her, it gently crawled into bed and laid next to her, listening to her heartbeat . . .

she could smell it

could feel its coarse hair

its warm breath

Climbing up toward consciousness, she wrestled with the bedsheets, the animal still clinging to her, hugging her to its bosom.

Carolyn fumbled for the bedside lamp and snapped it on. The light was harsh, throwing shadows to the far corners of the room. She sat there listening to the sound of her own breathing.

Shocked and ashamed, she realized she had wet the bed.

CHAPTER THIRTEEN

Harrison Chee awoke to the sound of wind shrieking past his hogan and leaking in through holes in the roof and walls. He heard a faint whisper in its wake, calling his name. During brief lulls in the windstorm came the sound of a coyote's yap. Chee closed his eyes again and pulled the thin blanket up to his chin, inviting sleep.

It was then that he heard the roof creak above his head.

At once his eyes flew open.

He stared upward into the darkness. Timbers moaned.

Chee yanked back his blanket, threw his feet over the side of the cot and listened. It was the footsteps of the devil, not below the earth, but up above, on his roof. He struck a match, turned up the lantern's wick, and lit it. The light spread gently.

Above him, the roof moaned like a wounded animal. Chee knew what was up there. It had come back again, this time to drop corpse powder through the smoke hole in the center of the hogan. He looked up in horror, expecting to see the magic potion drift downward at any moment; his heart pounded as he saw the ceiling boards bend inward; he heard another step, much louder, and realized the wolf wasn't even trying to be quiet. It moved again. Chee followed its progress by watching the boards above bow dangerously taut—the thing had to weigh upward of two hundred pounds. Squeaking wood marked its path. The roof was weak; Chee feared the creature's weight would bring it crashing down.

The sounds stopped again. There was a brief rush of wind, and in the quiet that followed Chee groped for his rifle. Finding it, he pulled back the bolt to ensure that it was loaded, then clicked it shut. Ice formed in his stomach, in his lungs, and inside his chest.

Get away! Chee screamed inwardly. *Go back to hell!*

The animal didn't move. Chee's heart almost stopped. He sensed the creature was reading his every thought, feeding off his fear. He strained to hear something. *Anything.*

There was only the low moan of the wind, but he suddenly shivered as an aching cold passed through his bones. He looked up toward the door just as it flew open. A blast of wind invaded his sanctuary, tossing the small objects in the room helter-skelter.

Chee almost screamed—almost—but his throat had closed. He clutched the .22 in a death grip but was unable to lift it; his muscles had turned to putty.

Touched by moonlight, the large figure outside moved into the doorway. It was shrouded in a wolf's skin, forepaws dangling near its chest. Crowned with an animal's empty skull, the face below was that of a man. Dried mud coated the features, and all Chee could see was the yellow glare of his eyes. His crusted lips seemed to wear a half smile, half sneer.

Suddenly, a wet sound that was supposed to be a laugh came out of its mouth.

"What are you going to do, you old fool, shoot me?" The voice was cracked and scratchy, barely above a whisper.

Chee worked his lips, trying to swallow something in his throat.

"Listen to me," the wolf commanded. "I've run out of patience with you. The *chindi* whose gold you stole cry out to me. Your brother Tyrone is still tormented by your greed—his *chindi* roams aimlessly in the great void, waiting for you to return the coins to the rightful owners."

"Return the coins?" Chee croaked. "But . . . "

"In a fortnight I'll be back. You could call it paying my respects: it will mark fifty years since your brother's death, you know. It will be a night with no moon, the Dark Night. You will come with me to return the coins to the Dead."

The wolf approached Chee, holding out another gold coin. The old man reached out for it, trembling, but the wolf slowly shook his head, his cruel mouth slit into a grimace. He raised the coin to Chee's lips. Chee suddenly remembered his youthful days at boarding school. He remembered attending mass on Sundays, where the priest would offer Holy Communion. Father Bennett would place a wafer on his tongue . . .

The wolf pressed the coin between Chee's lips in mockery.

"Take . . . eat, you fool. This is *my* body. This is *my*

blood. You will give the coins back to the Dead from whence they came. Remember, fourteen nights."

Chee nodded. His skin felt like it was covered with countless tiny worms.

"Very good. I hope you'll forgive this interruption tonight."

Again Chee nodded.

"Good. And I believe it would be best not to mention our little discussion to anyone. We wouldn't want any more accidents, would we?"

Chee shook his head, mesmerized by the scratchy whisper.

The wolf offered a deadly smile, then held out a pint of whiskey. "I'll be going now. Try to calm yourself. You'll only have to see me one last time. *Hágoónee.*"

PART III

Yellow/Twilight

CHAPTER FOURTEEN

The weather was blustery. Low clouds hugged the mesas, covering their flat tops in fluffy gauze. A gray tint in the landscape filled the ravines. Gusts of wind whistled through the piñons and caused the trees to shiver like blackbirds taking flight. Farther west, purple thunderheads slowly built up, massing together like an army. Jesse studied the dark clouds for a moment, then returned his attention to the block of stone mounted in the barrel. It had remained untouched for a week now while he thought about what he wanted to carve out of the chunk of rock.

The general form would be blocked out this morning, the outer layers removed gradually and evenly until the sleepy figure inside emerged. It was a slow process that required patience. Eventually it would become the head of a child, a boy whose neck and small shoulders would strain to lift themselves out of the mass of sandstone. Jesse rarely carved the entire figure away from the stone. He preferred to leave an unfinished area, not allowing the form complete freedom from its shell. It had become his trademark, part of the style he had developed over the dozen or so pieces he'd carved since beginning to work in stone.

His love for sculpture began in fifth grade, after a visit to the Albuquerque Museum on a school field trip. Something inside him had softly cried *Yes! This is what I have to do.* He had stood in awe of the towering Indian figures sculpted by R. C. Gorman; he had run his fingers along the small head of a boy carved out of granite by the great sculptor John Flanagan; he had marveled at the mystery of the abstract shape carved by Henry Moore. It had been like absorbing another person's passion, lighting fires in his own soul. The visual effects were exciting; the heaviness of the medium itself seemed to call out to him. As the other kids laughed and frolicked through the sculpture garden, Jesse had felt as though he were walking on sacred ground.

Afterward, Jesse began borrowing large quantities of art books from the Gallup Public Library, pouring over everything he could find on sculpture. He learned about the colossus of granite carved in ancient Egypt, the graceful works in marble sculpted by Michelangelo. Jesse read about the contemporaries: Constantin Brancusi, Henry Moore, and Isamu Noguchi. He pondered the modern abstractions, concluding they were simplifications that tried to capture the inner spirit of the objects they represented. He understood this, yet would never have been able to explain it to someone else.

He also started collecting books describing the methods of sculpture: the tools needed, materials used, the stones that could be carved. After talking his father into buying him a mallet and chisel, Jesse began hacking away at various rocks. Although he had many minor injuries to his thumb and knuckles from misguided hammer blows, he eventually gained skill in carving. The first sculptures were crude, but it was obvious to everyone, including Jesse, that there was a natural talent here, one that only needed hours and hours of practice to perfect. Like horseback riding or basketball, the more he did it, the better he got.

When his mom and dad realized that he meant to stick with his newfound craft, they supported him wholeheartedly, purchasing more tools and encouraging him. The long lonely hours after school and on summer vacations were now occupied with finding boulders, hauling them, envisioning their inner forms, and painstakingly freeing that image from its covering. Some pieces were polished to a luster with files and emery cloth, others were left rough. Most were a combination, offering a contrast between the roughness of a surface in its natural state and the smoothness of a refined work. Jesse loved the tactile quality of sculpture almost as much as its visual impact. Textural contrasts, showing the marks of chisel and hammer, excited him as much as the areas polished smooth as glass.

And surprisingly, after only a couple of years of sculpting, he had been able to begin selling a piece here and there. Several trading posts now stocked his work, and tourists were buying it. Profits were split fifty-fifty with the stores, providing Jesse with enough pocket money that he seldom had to rely on his mom for school clothes, tools, or anything else he needed. Eventually, he hoped to make enough to help her with the bills as well.

The carport connected to the south end of the

trailer was Jesse's studio. Tools were hung neatly along one wall: bush hammers, mallets, toothed chisels, and points. His father had rigged up a block and tackle for moving heavier stones; it ran along the length of the ceiling beam. An assortment of odds and ends—sand-filled barrels containing unfinished sculptures, a shelf of art magazines, a box of loose sketches, chains, wooden skids—lined the south wall. The work space was cool in the summer; it blocked the wind well, and with the powerful overhead lights, Jesse could work late into the evening.

Jesse began to chip away at the new stone, roughing out the mass with a point chisel. With a short-handled mallet, he pounded the mushroomed end of the point in a two-one rhythm, flaking away superfluous areas. Although the morning was cool, he soon needed to tie a scarf around his head to keep the sweat out of his eyes. His plastic safety goggles fogged as he circled the barrel on which the boulder rested, striking here and there with calculated blows.

Two hours later he put down his tools, pulled off the scarf and safety glasses, and ran a gloved hand over the stone. The sharp edges had been hewn away; the bulk of the surface was ready to be reduced further with the bush hammer. The metallic teeth of the hammer would wear down the surface by pulverization more precisely than the point.

It was time for a walk. Jesse did his best thinking while walking, especially after allowing his mind to free itself of worries while sculpting. He wiped his face with the scarf and stuffed it into his back pocket before taking a swig of water from the plastic jug. He could hear his mother preparing breakfast, so he set off for his hike only after hollering through the screen door that he would be back within half an hour.

"Not any longer," his mother's voice carried out to him between the rattle of pots and pans.

She had been upset over the horse incident. Although she had believed him when he explained to Clah how he happened to have the horse, she worried that it might cost her her job at the store. Fortunately, the new owner never mentioned a word about it, so the trouble seemed to have blown over. Clah came back the day after they picked up the horse to let them know that the Manchesters weren't going to press charges. His mother had been visibly relieved, but Jesse had merely shrugged it off. *So kind of them,* he thought. It was a wild accusation, anyway. Who in their right mind would steal a horse, ride it all over the country in broad daylight, then pen it up right at their home, within four miles of where it had been stolen? Obviously, the horse had simply broken loose; the *bilagáanas* hadn't been smart enough to corral it properly.

And that girl was something else. He smiled to himself as he pictured her blasting him with those scornful eyes. If looks could kill, he'd be nothing more than a memory. She was extremely pretty, no doubt, but really stuck on herself, like most good-looking girls, especially *bilagáanas.*

At his mother's prodding, Jesse had almost gone over to the store the following day to explain to the Manchesters how he happened to have the horse, but then he decided against it. It wouldn't have done any good; they had already made up their minds that he was a thief and a stupid one at that.

The girl's angry looks proved it. Let them think whatever they wanted. Funny thing was even Clah seemed to side with them. He didn't say so, but Jesse had sensed it by the way he had handled everything. The wayward son after the father's death. *Thanks a lot, Clah, for your vote of confidence in me. Dad would appreciate it.*

And then there was the question of whether he had been sneaking around, peeking into their windows, like he was some kind of pervert. Fine. Let 'em think it. He'd just make sure he never set foot in that store again. The Ramah Trading Post was only another twelve miles down the road; he would do his business there.

Thinking about the store led to another concern: his grandfather. A week ago his mother had discovered the old man lying in bed in a fetal position, almost catatonic. He couldn't sit up or speak or even move. She had driven to Red Rock and called an ambulance. His grandfather was taken to Gallup, where the doctor said he had suffered a small stroke. He had spent five days there and finally came home yesterday.

The old man didn't look as bad now as he had the first couple of days in the hospital, but that wasn't saying much. He seemed more frail than ever. His skin hung like loose fabric on his bones; his eyes were empty and sunken. When he spoke, it was in a hoarse whisper. But most oddly of all, his mother had told him that she had found the old man clutching one of the large gold coins he'd shown him earlier, squeezing it to his breast in a death grip. The nurses literally had to pry it out of his fingers.

Jesse checked his watch, turned around on the path, and headed back. Wind rattled through the trees, sending short shocks through the branches. His loose-fitting shirt fluttered against his body. Clouds raced low overhead. He would go visit his grandfather again today, he decided. Maybe show him his coin. He had to wring more information out of the old man. There was something sinister about the coins, and he had to find out just what they were and where they came from. Why had his father had one in his possession the night he died? Did they have anything to do with his *accident?*

All anyone seemed to know about his father's death was that he had been in an auto accident. He had officially been off duty, his shift ending at six in the evening. The accident was estimated to have happened around two or three the following morning. No one had any idea why Franklin Begay had still been in uniform, or why he had still been out in the police carry-all at those hours. According to Clah, his father hadn't mentioned anything about any after-hours follow-up, although Jesse's mom said he had told her there was something he needed to check on that evening, something that was probably nothing more than a kid's prank. He said he'd be home shortly. Jesse's father left at dusk and never came home again.

And somehow the coins had something to do with it, Jesse was certain. But *what*? Where did they come from? His grandfather said he had stolen them many years ago from Broken Bones. Who was Broken Bones?

And then the old man claimed that he had returned them to the dead, that he had put them in the coffin with his younger brother Tyrone. So how did Jesse's father happen to have one? And then there was the skin-walker. Grandfather claimed he had seen it, had spoken to it, had even shot at it. Jesse himself had felt its presence that morning, something evil lurking beyond the trees; it hadn't been his imagination. *Something* had been out there, watching and waiting. And now Jesse was sure that the coins had something to do with his grandfather's stroke. Had the old man received another coin that night? Had he again seen the witch? How did the death of Jesse's father fit into all this? There were too many questions, too many loose ends writhing like snakes in a pit. He had to go see his grandfather again; he had to get some answers.

Jesse's mother was putting eggs and bacon on the table just as he came through the door. Perfect timing. The toaster popped up in greeting, and Sadie Begay smiled brightly at her son. "Go wash up. Breakfast is ready."

"Smells great."

She beamed at him, and his heart suddenly hurt. He knew that he was her jewel, the tiny spark that kept her heart alive from day to day. Whenever he thought about his father, he could feel his mother's pain deep inside his chest, a pressure that crushed his heart and lungs together.

He returned to the tiny dining room, sat down at the table, and began piling food on his plate. His mother pulled off her apron and sat across from him.

"I've made some loaves of bread I want you to take

to Grandpa today, okay?" She buttered a piece of toast and balanced it on Jesse's plate. "You can drive me to work so you can have the truck."

"That's okay," Jesse muttered through a mouthful of eggs. "I'll ride over. I'll carry it in my saddlebags."

"Just don't squish it. Make sure he's eating and taking his medicine. I've written out what he's supposed to be taking and how much. I'll put it in the bag with the bread. Also, ask him when he wants to go to the store, or if he'd rather go into town. The doctor said he needs to get out more often."

Jesse nodded between gulps. "What time you going to be home?" he asked, forking another piece of egg to his mouth.

"Around eight, like usual. Why?"

"No reason. Just wondered."

Ever since his father had died, Jesse had begun watching over his mother more closely, taking on a role more like her big brother than her son. He was protective, watchful of her comings and goings, her time away. It was kind of obsessive, he knew, so he rarely even admitted to himself that he was doing it.

"Also, let me know if you think he's still drinking," his mother added. "The doctor said he has to stop, his heart can't take it. If you think he's still at it, I'm going to call Clah and ask him to put some pressure on the local bootleggers to stay away. I'd love to see them all thrown in jail."

She poured more milk in his glass, filling it to the brim.

Jesse didn't say anything. Of course his grandfather

was still drinking. He wondered what he should tell his mom when he came back. He figured if the bottle was taken away from the old man this late in the game, it would surely kill him, just as fast as any stroke. The doctors would know that, too, but what else could they say?

"There's roast beef for lunch and some leftover potato salad. You want me to make you sandwiches?"

Jesse smiled. "Thanks. But I'll do it. Leave the dishes for me, too, okay? I'll go saddle Smiley. Who knows, maybe along the way I'll be lucky enough to find another horse." He winked at her.

The look from his mother said she didn't think he was very funny.

CHAPTER FIFTEEN

Carolyn hoisted herself up into the saddle, swinging her English riding boot over the gelding and into a stirrup. Nakai sidestepped automatically, but Harlan Mitchell held the halter firmly, handing the reins to Carolyn.

"He's feeling frisky this morning," Harlan said. The corners of his eyes crinkled into an expression close to a smile.

"Always," Carolyn quipped. "I don't think he has a calm bone in his body." The horse pranced spryly to illustrate her point. Harlan strolled over to the gate, opened it, and waved her through. "Be careful in the arroyos," he cautioned. "The sand is deep and could cause your horse to trip."

"I will. Thanks."

"Another thing."

Carolyn held in Nakai with effort, peering down at Harlan.

"Keep your bearings straight—it's easy to get lost out there. Rocks and trees can begin to all look alike. The terrain can fool you. Do you have a canteen?"

She nodded and pointed at her saddlebags, anxious now to have free rein. But Harlan held on for a moment longer, eliciting eye contact. His eyes were dark doors where she didn't wish to enter. He finally released the halter and ushered her out of the gate. Carolyn waved and galloped across the field; she looked back once and Harlan was still there.

Nakai instantly picked up speed and she allowed him his head. The ground below slipped away like a video on fast forward; she crouched low over her horse, lost in the thoroughbred's mane as he crossed the land with great strides. Carolyn's ponytail blew straight back in the wind; her large shirt fluttered against her like the flapping of tiny wings.

For the past week, Carolyn's rides on Nakai had become daily routine. She loved the freedom she felt on the magnificent horse, and she could sense that Nakai looked forward to it too. Gone were the days of his testing her skills as a rider, testing to see who would master whom. The rearing, bucking, and spinning had ceased.

Gone, too, were the initial feelings of alienation that Carolyn had felt when she had arrived at Red Rock. She was growing accustomed to the remoteness, to the austere old Navajos who piled out of the back of the pickup trucks at her father's store; to the unrestrained, impish children who accompanied them, giggling and laughing as they ran about. The Navajos were warm and friendly once you got to know them, unpretentious, and surprisingly accepting of outsiders like herself. By spending a few hours a day in the store helping her father, she had already come to know quite a lot of people, but unfortunately none were her own age.

Her mother now spent at least half of each day pecking at her computer, and her father worked at the store from seven-thirty in the morning until eight at night. This left too many hours for Carolyn to entertain herself, and even the time spent grooming and caring for her horse didn't dispel the feelings of loneliness that often crept up on her. She had already read three novels and written a slew of letters to friends back East, just to fill in time.

She had never mentioned anything to her parents about going back to Boston as she had planned, aware that Nakai was an effective bribe to keep her contented for the summer. Her dad promised he'd ship the horse back to Winston Heath Livery when she returned to Boston at the end of summer break. So although she was lonely, she figured she could endure the reservation for another ten weeks. Perhaps she would make friends with some of the kids out here, she told herself. They couldn't be that different from her friends back home, could they?

The bizarre incidents of her first night on the rez had pretty much faded in memory. She'd concluded she had probably dreamt it, or if there had been someone at her window, her imagination had embellished what she had actually seen. Witches, bogey men, were only stories to scare children, superstitious nonsense. If someone had been at her window, it had most likely been that strange boy who had stolen her horse; he had probably been creeping around, seeing what else he could get his hands on. Her scream had probably scared him more than he had frightened her. Anyway, skinwalkers or whatever they were no longer held her in fear, and she doubted if anything so weird really existed. Nevertheless, the ghost beads given to her by Harlan Mitchell still hung around her neck.

Carolyn reined in Nakai, shifted her weight, and

coaxed him down a steep embankment. The wind would be less blustery down in the arroyo, which was sheltered by trees. Gray clouds trailed tendrils of showers over the distant mesas and were heading her way; dark green stands of piñon glimmered in the hazy light. The extent of her solitariness spread over her just then, causing a shiver down her spine. Except for the creaking of her saddle and Nakai's hooves on an occasional rock, the only other sound was the wind.

A feeling grew in her that she was being watched, a feeling of eyes on her. Irrationally, the sensation became stronger: The mouse became a beast, something baleful and immense and savage. Carolyn had never felt such terror. And it was as much despair as fear, an utter and complete hopelessness.

In the blanket of gray shadows, a creature followed her with its eyes. She rode on, feeling it claiming her from its hiding place in the rocks or behind the trees. The touch of those eyes made her feel dirty, soiled in some way that couldn't be defined. As she and Nakai moved up and out of the ravine and again secured level ground, Carolyn nudged the horse into a faster gait.

The thing, whatever it was, moved with her, sliding through the shadows on her left. At times it lagged behind, then melted into the haze and passed among the trees, moving effortlessly ahead of her. She felt its gaze on her face, caressing her cheek with its foul touch.

Carolyn's heart fluttered like a butterfly in her chest. She forced herself not to panic. She had to figure out what to do. There was open land ahead; should she make a dash and hope to lose the thing stalking her?

Would she be intercepted? An image formed in her mind of a rabid wolf darting across the meadow, faster even than her Nakai, its teeth bared and eyes crazed with blood lust . . . she shook the picture away and, as nonchalantly as possible, peered over her shoulder. Should she turn around and ride back the way she had come? Would the thing out there let her go home?

Your imagination's getting the best of you, Cara. Nothing out there but grasshoppers and lizards. No. Whatever it was, it was there, and it was close. She clutched the ghost beads in one hand, gripping her reins tightly in the other. Her anxiety was relayed to Nakai, who broke into a canter. In the open area ahead she would make a wide sweep to the right, pick up speed, then race toward home at a full run. She would give Nakai his head and let him cover the distance at whirlwind speed. They would fly.

"Come on, boy," she urged. "I need you now."

Nakai's muscles tightened. His ears laid back, and his powerful legs gathered speed; his stride became rhythmic.

A shrill whistle sounded from close behind, and suddenly a large black crow flapped out of a piñon in front of them. It swooped close, its caw ringing in Carolyn's ears. Nakai swerved and at the same instant a flurry of black birds erupted from another tree. Nakai reared.

And that was when she went down in the sand. The wind whooshed out of her as she landed on her back, and tiny lights twinkled and floated before her eyes. She lay there a moment, dazed, staring up at the clouds. Her heart thudded in her temples, and she wanted to cry. She moved one leg, then the other, then her arms. Surprisingly, everything worked without too much pain, thanks to the soft cushioning of sand. Even her eyeglasses, which were lying nearby, had miraculously remained intact.

She sat up slowly, combed the sand and sticks out of her hair with her fingers, then put her glasses back on. A dull ache centered itself between her shoulder blades. Carolyn looked around, searching for Nakai. She spotted him about a hundred yards away, watching her and prodding the ground nervously with a hoof. She called out to him, but he refused to come nearer.

Determined to force her wobbly legs to support her, Carolyn stood and fixed her gaze on the rocks and trees from which the whistle had come. It was still out there, she was certain, and now she was on foot. Anger replaced fear. She searched the ground for a weapon. Anything—a rock or a big stick would do.

Lightning double-flashed in the distance, and the smell of fresh rain and pine came to her nostrils. She picked up a large stone and stood there waiting, watching the rain clouds cross the mesas and swathe the treetops like angel's hair. Nakai inched a few steps closer but was still reluctant to come too close to the trees. Behind her, she heard hoofbeats.

The sound shocked her; her pulse rioting, she whirled around. Everything was a blur, jerking and stretching. Then she recognized the boy who had stolen her horse.

He slowed his mount and approached warily. When he was within throwing distance of Nakai, he reined in his animal and lightly slid out of his saddle with the absentminded ease that comes only from years of riding.

Carolyn felt helpless as he walked over to Nakai, gathered the reins without as much as a blink of resistance from him, and walked both horses toward her.

Thunder rolled from somewhere behind her. The boy looked at Carolyn with a careful absence of expression; the only animation was in his eyes, which seemed to scrutinize everything. Long strands of black hair had escaped the tie at the nape of his neck and blew like coils of smoke in front of his face. Carolyn dropped her rock, feeling both self-conscious and foolish.

"You lost something," he said, handing her Nakai's reins.

"Thanks," she managed to mutter.

"What were you going to do with that?" he asked, gesturing with his eyes toward the rock. "Hit 'em with it?"

"Not him—you," she countered, never to be outwitted in a duel of words.

The movement that flicked across his face was too small to be called a smile. "That's funny," he conceded. "You're a real funny girl."

Carolyn felt an unwilling grin stretch her own mouth. "I try to be. And just for laughs, why don't you tell me why you're following me."

He studied her for a moment, then said something in Navajo.

"What?"

"I said you're crazy."

Carolyn tried to look indifferent. "How nice." She brushed the dirt off her arms and shoulders and pulled Nakai close.

"You all right?" he asked, his voice almost gentle now.

"Yeah. It's not the first time I've been thrown, and probably not the last."

"Maybe you need some riding lessons," he said.

Carolyn's jaw dropped open, and for an instant she was at a loss how to reply. She felt her anger mounting.

"Maybe. And maybe you need to be locked up for stealing my horse. Maybe you need to see a psychiatrist about being a Peeping Tom. And maybe, just maybe, you ought to be a little less quick to judge a situation."

She yanked Nakai away, tightened the cinch around his girth, and was about to mount.

"I think you ought to follow your own advice. I never stole your horse. And I might need a psychiatrist, but I'm no Peeping Tom."

"So what are you going to tell me, that it wasn't you that I saw at my window, that it was a *skinwalker?* I've already heard that." And at the moment, she was prone to believe it.

The boy's complexion grew ashen, and he muttered something in Navajo.

"Huh?"

"What do you know about a *yee naaldlooshii*, a skinwalker?"

"Enough," she replied prudently.

A strange flicker danced in the boy's eyes. *"Digis bilagáana."*

"What?" She found herself asking again, annoyed with his game of speaking to her in a tongue she didn't understand, and worse, playing into it with *"Huh?"* and *"What?"*

No answer, of course. Obstinate boy.

116

Lightning again flashed in the grayness behind her. She could feel the static and smell the ozone in the air. "I'd best be getting home," she said as she swung up into her saddle. Nakai tossed his head up and down nervously. "I think it's gone now."

"What's gone?"

"Never mind."

"Fine."

Carolyn looked down at him with a gaze she normally reserved for the most foolish boys at her school. Nakai pranced in skittish sidesteps as lightning stabbed through the clouds, this time nearby, followed by a loud crack of thunder. A scarf of cool wind carried moisture. She watched the boy shake his head, then remount. For some reason, she reined in Nakai, hesitant to leave even with the threat of the downpour. He rode over to her, and she sensed that he too was in no hurry to ride away. His mare wrestled with the reins, but he held her in check inattentively, his movements an extension of the animal's motion. Carolyn was keenly aware of the physical attraction she was feeling toward this peculiar boy.

When he rode up close to her, as close as the two horses would allow, Nakai snorted and shook his head in protest. The lightning flashed at what seemed within touching distance away and was followed by another explosion of thunder.

"Ride down the arroyo over there until you get to the trees," he said, pointing. "Then cut through where it starts getting rocky. You'll see a sheep trail that will lead you back to the trading post. You might even make it most of the way back before you get drenched. *Hágoónee,* funny girl."

In a few seconds he'd be gone, Carolyn realized. In a few seconds she would be alone again. The thought made her stomach tighten. "Wait!" she cried.

He pulled in his reins as the chestnut was about to leap away, causing his horse to rear.

"Don't go, yet," Carolyn expelled. "I . . . I'm afraid something might happen to me. Something's out there . . . I'm in danger."

The boy steadied his horse and arched an eyebrow, waiting to hear more.

"Before you rode up, I swear something was following me—I could feel it. Something spooked my horse, and that's how I took my spill. I think it might be a skinwalker." Carolyn spewed it all out like a confession, afraid that the boy might ride away and abandon her to whatever was stalking her; she fought down the panic. That was the strength of evil, she saw: its absence of hope, its stink of despair. She didn't want to face whatever was out there alone. The thing that she had seen at her window one night now repeated itself in the haunted house of her mind.

"I'm afraid," she said in a whisper, unsure if the words could even be heard, if she wanted them heard. They were the two most difficult words she had ever spoken.

He looked at her for a long moment, his eyes studying hers. "I hunt the *yee naaldlooshii*. I will ride with you."

He pulled at a long leather sheath attached to his saddlebags, and Carolyn only then realized that he was carrying a firearm. He unsnapped the flap, exposing the wooden butt of a rifle. A large raindrop plopped on her forehead, and the wind threw sand in her face.

The boy led the way at a gallop. It began to rain.

CHAPTER SIXTEEN

She looked around the kitchen and realized that things were exactly as they had been a few hours ago. Merely hours ago! It seemed like days. The rainstorm had left her sopping, but it had already passed. After tending Nakai, she had showered and changed into something dry and was now amazed to find the weather already changing. The evening sun peeked through the clouds, lacing the thick cumulus with shades of pink. The billowy mass scudded across her window view as Carolyn's mind replayed the details of her encounter with Sadie Begay's son.

His name was Jesse; she remembered hearing it from either her father or from the Navajo cop. Did he know her name? Most likely. She realized her opinion of him had changed radically, especially since he had escorted her nearly all the way home. They hadn't talked, but, rather, rode silently in single file on the narrow, rain-slicked trail, enduring the rain's harsh pelting. When the trading post had finally come into view, he turned his mount around, nodded curtly, and rode away. She couldn't recall if she had thanked him or not.

Her interest in him was simply because she was lonely for a friend her own age—it had nothing to do with the fact that he was good-looking. Carolyn told herself this more than once and wondered when she'd see him again. A twinge of guilt reminded her of Thomas. She was his girl, sort of.

After opening and closing the fridge twice, she decided to make a salad. She pulled out a tired head of lettuce and began tearing it into small pieces in a bowl. She wasn't hungry, but since neither parent was home, it gave her something to do. It also occupied her so she wouldn't think about the experience she had while riding today. At least, she hoped it would.

The pain between her shoulder blades reminded her of the hard spill she had taken. Were there really such things as skinwalkers? Should she tell her parents that she had felt she was being stalked? Was she that certain it hadn't simply been manifestations of some of her own fears gurgling to the surface of her consciousness, playing tricks with her mind? She had had psychology classes this past year and had read of such instances. Mr. Greene, her psychology teacher, would have logical, scientific explanations for all this: Her subconscious fears were surfacing due to her unfamiliar surroundings, ancient archetypal symbols were manifesting through her dreams; or maybe it was all some Fruedian sexual thing. And she had a few of her own skeptical theories: Little City Girl Lost in the Big Bad Woods was one. She felt foolish for telling the boy she had been afraid. What did he think of her? First she tries to have him arrested, then she cries out to him for help. Did he believe her about being stalked? He hadn't laughed or scorned her; actually, his expression had communicated his belief.

Or had he merely felt sorry for her, felt he needed to help the little girl find her way home?

Tired of mulling it over, Carolyn gave up on the salad and started searching for aspirin instead. A dull throb had settled at her temples and down her back. She was lucky she hadn't been hurt worse. Searching cabinets proved futile; she'd have to run over to the store. And since her father owned it, would she have to pay? She stuffed a five from the cookie jar into her pocket, just in case.

Leaving the house, she was struck full in the face by the fresh scent of pine and damp earth. Sidestepping puddles and tiptoeing over the muddy spots, Carolyn crossed the nearly empty parking lot toward the store. Mauve clouds turned purple as the sun descended over the silhouetted buttes in the west; large black crows careened across a smattering of piñons. The memory of crows bounced in her brain. She still heard the shrill whistle, felt the presence of evil. It made her shudder.

She waved at Lena when she entered the trading post, but Lena was preoccupied with a customer. Carolyn passed the canned goods and cereals, moving toward shelves of tonics and balms. She found a familiar brand, turned, and headed toward Lena's counter. Should she pay, or simply show Lena the box?

Tullie was stocking a shelf near the end of her aisle, his back to her, and Carolyn realized she would have to walk past him. Recollections of him scowling at her made her apprehensive; she held her breath as she passed him, expecting a repeat of last week's episode at any second. Either he didn't notice her or he was acting as if he didn't, which allowed Carolyn a sigh of relief.

Free sailing.

But there was something wrong.

Carolyn glanced over her shoulder; Tullie was still hunched over a stack of boxes, avoiding her. *Something wrong.*

Another glance.

The floor.

Tullie stood on legs as thick as tree stumps. His boots were encrusted with grime all the way up his pantlegs to his knees. His clothes—a denim jacket and worn jeans—were soaked.

Carolyn's first impulse was to alert Tullie to the mess he was making of her father's newly refinished floor. "Tullie, look at your boots!"

Tullie spun around, his face a mask.

Regretting that she had sounded as if she were scolding him, Carolyn pointed at his feet. Tullie looked down at the muddied floor, then snapped a glare back at Carolyn, challenging her with a cold stare.

"Dad just refinished the floor," she blurted, trying to take the edge off her earlier reprimand. At that moment she felt more aware of her youth than ever, realizing the rule she had violated, the taboo which spanned cultures: A young person does not reprove an adult.

"Don't worry yourself over it, little *ach'j'nahwii'ná.*" Tullie's voice had the quality of a wood rasp drawn across a metal can. He turned around and resumed his work.

Carolyn wanted to ask how on earth he had gotten so filthy and wet, but she had already said too much. Maybe she should get a mop and clean up, try

122

to dissipate some of the hostility she had caused. She changed her mind abruptly when Tullie turned once more and spat something at her in Navajo, expelling the words from his mouth as if they were rotten meat. Carolyn didn't have a clue as to what he had said to her, and she didn't want to know. She backed off immediately.

Suddenly her heart contracted. Her mind skittered.

Tullie had been out in the rain. On foot. In the rain. In the woods.

She almost knocked over a wobbly candy stand as she fumbled toward the front of the store. Nausea began to rise in her throat and she swallowed hard, driving it down. Tullie. He had been out there. The scene of something sliding through the shadows, watching her, following her, printed itself with utter clarity on her mind. She turned around again, but Tullie was out of sight, hidden behind rows and rows of cans, condiments, boxes and boxes, all of which spun in a whirling merry-go-round of abstract shapes, blurring and darkening, beginning to tilt . . .

When she bumped to a halt, Carolyn caught her breath and stared up at her father's face: a million pained expressions. "Cara. For God's sake, what's the matter with you?"

She blinked, tried to summon a reply. She felt her father's hand on her forehead.

"You sick? You're perspiring."

"I . . . I'm fine," she finally stammered. "Just a headache. I got caught out in the rain with Nakai. I'm all right."

Her father didn't look convinced. She noticed that

he was looking down at the small box in her hand—the aspirin. She held it up. "Should I pay for this?"

He shook his head. "Go home and rest. Your mother and I will be home shortly . . ."

"Dad, how come Tullie's all wet?"

Her father regarded her in an odd manner.

"His boots are all muddy. He's tracking up all over your floor."

Jack Manchester stared at his daughter with an expression that suggested she might need an interpreter, or maybe a psychiatrist. Wrinkles creased vertically along his forehead. "Tullie?" He glanced back in Tullie's direction.

She nodded. "He was out in the rain."

"Uh-huh. So? He was putting in new fenceposts. We're going to build a higher fence for Nakai, make sure your horse doesn't do any more disappearing acts. Apparently, Tullie got caught in the rain. Said his truck is stuck out there and he had to walk back to the store. Unfortunately, we don't have any dry clothes around here that will fit him. Harlan offered to give him a ride home tonight; we'll pull his truck out tomorrow, after it dries out a bit."

"Any mess that Tullie has made can be cleaned up, Cara. Don't worry yourself over such silly things."

Again she nodded, but wasn't convinced. Carolyn hadn't noticed any new fenceposts when she had ridden in. And she certainly hadn't seen any truck.

She went through the door, aware of her father's puzzled stare. She was tired, and her headache was getting worse.

▼

Sunshine came through the front windows in warm, slanted columns, taking the edge off the morning's crispness and illuminating the countless specks of dust, glittering fairy powder. Carolyn smiled, bagged groceries, and handed them to a customer. The woman reciprocated with a smile, thanking her in Navajo: *"Ahéhéé."*

"Aó," Carolyn returned, pushing her glasses up and brushing hair away from her face. Her eyes shone; the tiredness was gone, along with her headache. The area between her shoulders still ached, but she could live with that. And for the moment, she had forgotten about her rendezvous with evil out on yesterday's ride, and about Tullie.

Her father had been shorthanded this morning, Charlotte had the day off, Lena hadn't shown up yet, and her mother had left early to spend the day working on some research in the Gallup library. Carolyn had wanted to tag along just to get away for the day, but her father asked her to fill in for awhile at the store; he promised her it would only be for the morning.

Which was fine, except that her coworker at the till was Sadie Begay. It made conversation awkward at best, impossible at worst. Sadie's manner toward her was polite but cool, the breech over the incident with her son and Nakai an obvious snag in their relationship. The worst of it was Carolyn now doubted if Nakai had been stolen; most likely, she had been wrong.

Last night Carolyn had asked her father about Tullie, trying not to sound anything more than curious. She had decided not to tell her parents about the danger she felt during her ride; they would either think she was being melodramatic, for she had no hard facts to prove she had actually been in danger, or they might go to the other extreme—forbidding her to ride alone—and she couldn't bear that. After a few questions of his own regarding how she was feeling, and Carolyn's assurance that she was feeling better, her father had told her that Tullie lived alone in a ramshackle hogan, without electricity, plumbing, or any other connection to the outside world. He was a hard worker, dependable, yet withdrawn. Her father had heard that he had been married once upon a time, but a terrible car accident many years ago had claimed the lives of his wife and two children. The Navajos were reluctant to talk about it.

Carolyn had felt sorry for him when she heard about the tragedy, but it didn't soothe her suspicions: Tullie was too weird, too blatantly hostile. Why did he seem to hate her so?

There was a lull between customers, and Carolyn found it especially uncomfortable. Sadie busied herself with picking up abandoned receipts and tiny scraps of paper that littered the area around the cash register; she wadded them into tiny balls and tossed them into the trash can, "the circular file," as her father called it. Carolyn watched, paced back and forth from the till to the front door, glanced at her watch, read for the third or fourth time the few hand-scratched notices tacked to the bulletin board, and contemplated what to say to the mother of that strange boy—the boy she had seen just yesterday and now wanted to see again.

"Mornings are usually busier than this," Sadie offered. "It will probably pick up in a little while."

"Dad should move some chairs up here so we could sit down when no one is around. Standing here all day would kill my feet."

Sadie smiled. Communication threatened to lapse into silence once again, and Carolyn felt she was being tortured.

"I saw your son yesterday. Did he tell you?"

Sadie's expression indicated that he hadn't.

"I was out riding, and my horse got spooked," she explained. "I was thrown, and your son happened to come by. He rounded up Nakai for me. I don't know if I thanked him or not—I was pretty shaken up from the spill. You wouldn't believe how glad I was that he showed up."

Sadie nodded. "He's like that, seems to always be there when there's a need."

"He's a good rider," Carolyn acknowledged. She could feel the stress in their communication waning; Jesse was a common point that could keep the conversation moving along. "I've seen few riders that can handle a horse like he does. He's looks so natural and at ease as he rides."

"His father taught him well."

"He must be a great horseman then. Does he train horses?"

Sadie averted her eyes. "Jesse's father died last summer."

"Oh. I'm sorry," Carolyn stammered, unsure of what to say and wishing for a sudden slew of customers. "How . . . I mean, what . . ."

"A car accident," Sadie replied flatly, attempting to

keep the emotion out of her voice. "He was a police-man. Jesse is a lot like him: too serious, too protective, too responsible. Like I said, his father taught him well."

Carolyn's breakfast rolled in her stomach. Why hadn't anyone told her this before? She thought about the accusations she had made against the boy a week ago, the certainty she had felt that he was guilty of steal-ing Nakai. A certainty she no longer held. Deep in her heart she knew she had judged the boy unfairly. Sadie and Jesse had every right to dislike her. "I think I was wrong accusing Jesse of stealing Nakai . . ."

Sadie watched Carolyn struggle with the most dif-ficult words in her vocabulary: "I . . . I'm sorry . . ." Sadie's smile seemed forced. "That's okay. My father always says 'Seeing something only after it's been pointed out to you is better than never seeing it at all.'"

A man wearing an old reservation-style Stetson approached the till, laid a new shovel on the counter, and asked for a tin of chewing tobacco. Sadie rang up the items as Carolyn puzzled over a plan to ride out and visit Jesse Begay. It would take some nerve on her part, but she and Jesse needed to talk.

CHAPTER SEVENTEEN

After lunch, Carolyn went toward Nakai's stable, equipped with Sadie's map and feeling confident that she could find her way to the Begay's home. Although she had been there once, she hadn't been sure she could remember which remote dirt road would take her there again. She walked past the rear corner of the store, cut across the parking lot, and considered what she would say to Jesse when she got there. Would he welcome her visit? Would he even be home? She wished more people out here had phones.

Looking toward the corner of the building, Carolyn squinted into the sunlight. Harlan and Spencer bobbed in and out of the shade of a large cottonwood. Spencer stood precariously balanced upon one of the uppermost rungs of a ladder; Harlan craned his neck, looking up toward Spencer's stocky figure. Sun dapples floated in and out of their work area.

"Good morning," she hailed, waving.

Spencer bent around awkwardly and smiled down at her, his face round and cheerful. *"Yá'át'ééh abíní."*

Harlan nodded, but his expression was, as usual, impossible to read.

Lena appeared at the back door and waved. "Where are you off to?"

Before Carolyn could answer, Lena shouted at the men. "Spencer, Mr. Manchester wants to see you."

"Tell him it will be a minute."

"He wants to see you now."

"I can't. I'm busy."

"It's about that *bilagáana* who wants to sell us hay out of Oklahoma," she persisted.

"Tell him I'll be in when I'm finished up here."

"You tell him," she said, slamming the door.

Harlan said something to Spencer in Navajo and both men laughed. Carolyn smiled. She didn't need an interpreter to get the gist of *that* remark. Harlan watched her for a moment, then said, "We've been providing the entertainment for your horse this morning. He's been watching Spencer wobbling around up here. I think he's been hoping our friend falls off." Carolyn laughed, then opened the gate as Nakai pranced over to greet her.

She saddled up and rode north past several hogans, then turned left onto a road that seemed vaguely familiar. Cheat grass fanned out almost as high as Nakai's shanks as he trotted between the tire ruts. Butterflies flitted in front of Carolyn as she kept a wary eye open for anything peculiar. Fortunately, she saw nothing out of the ordinary; her ride was pleasant and free of the threatening feeling she experienced on her last outing.

A half hour passed before she recognized a familiar landscape of junipers and rocky hillsides that suggested she was getting close to Jesse's home. When she reached the summit of a small knoll, Carolyn caught a glimpse of the Begay trailer nestled between hillocks below. She hoped that Jesse would be home and that her visit would be welcomed.

As she drew closer, Carolyn could see someone at the far end of the house, moving in and out of the shaded area of the carport; she was pretty sure it was Jesse. A dog barked, which caused the figure to turn around and notice her. He shielded his eyes with one hand and stood watching. She hoped it wasn't a mistake coming here. Would he be glad to see her, or would he give her a sullen look as he had a week ago?

The moment Jesse recognized Carolyn, he waved and began to wade through the tall grass toward her. The dog, still yapping madly, ran ahead, causing Nakai to prance skittishly. Jesse called out to the mongrel in Navajo but was ignored. Carolyn looked down at it and wondered how many years of crossbreeding it had taken to create such a ragged mutt.

"Hi," he greeted her cautiously. She noticed that he held a squarish hammer in one hand and his T-shirt and jeans were covered with a fine white dust.

"Hi. I hope I'm not interrupting anything," Carolyn said, sliding down from Nakai's back and gathering the reins loosely in her hand.

Jesse shook his head. "Nothing that can't wait." He watched her with feigned casualness. After an awkward moment of standing there looking at each other, they began to walk toward the house, Carolyn leading Nakai by the reins while the dog sniffed at her heels.

"You haven't introduced me to your friend," Carolyn said with a smile, watching that the dog wouldn't nip her.

Jesse looked back and shrugged. "I don't think he has a name."

"He isn't yours?"

"Not really. He just showed up several months ago, and we feed him. Then he's gone again. I guess he kinda lives here, but I wouldn't say we own him. He comes and goes as he pleases; he seldom follows me around like you'd expect a dog to do."

Jesse pointed over to the stable where his mare stood watching them approach. "You can tie your horse up back here. There's a water trough on the other side, and a bucket of fresh oats. He likes these oats, I remember." Jesse admired Nakai as she led him into the fenced area. "He's quite a beauty."

"Just don't forget who he belongs to," Carolyn chided. He gave her a sidelong glance. "You never quit, do you?"

"Uh-uh. It's a personality quirk prevalent among spoiled rich kids, especially kids from back East."

"I figured that."

As Carolyn took care of Nakai, Jesse put his hammer down and reknotted the red handkerchief around his head. His hair wasn't tied back today but hung loose over his shoulders. Carolyn had never seen hair so long on a boy.

"Let me go clean up," he said, swatting dust off his jeans. "I'll be back in a minute." He bounded the wooden steps to the back door and disappeared inside. The thin aluminum door smacked against the door frame, then drifted open.

Carolyn wandered over to where Jesse had been

working, curious about what he was fixing or building. What she saw surprised her.

The shape of a child struggled to free itself from a large block of stone. An assortment of chisels and other tools were scattered about, and fine dust and chunks of rock covered the cement floor. Another sculpture, somewhat smaller, stood in a barrel near the wall. It was a carving of a woman wrapped in a blanket, hands outstretched in an act of supplication. The smooth mass of the blanket was polished to a glow. In contrast, the hair that flowed down her back was rough, showing marks of the chisel Jesse had used to make it. It was beautiful—how could a boy her age create such beautiful things?

He came up behind her and smiled awkwardly.

"You made these?" she asked, instantly realizing what a dumb question that was. *No, Cara, Bugs Bunny did.*

Jesse merely nodded. "It keeps me out of trouble, most of the time."

She looked at him and caught the sparkle in his eyes.

"It's beautiful. Can I touch it?"

"Sure."

Carolyn ran her fingers over the stone, collecting a fine white dust on her fingertips.

"It's hard to believe that something this beautiful could actually be made out of rock," she exclaimed. "It must take forever."

"It takes a while," Jesse conceded. "You chisel away piece after piece, tearing it down. Creation is a destruction of sorts."

The thought behind that statement touched her.

She stared at him. "You sure you're not really an adult trapped inside a kid's body or something?"

Jesse laughed. "I'm fifteen. It's funny you'd say that—my dad used to say just about the same thing."

The mention of his father reminded Carolyn of the conversation she had had with Sadie that morning and the reason for her visit. It was time for a large helping of humble pie. "Look, I think I owe you an apology. I blamed you unfairly for stealing Nakai. I was probably wrong."

"Probably?"

"Yeah. I mean, no. I *was* wrong. I don't think you stole him. I probably shouldn't have been so quick to judge the situation."

"Probably?"

"Okay. Okay. I *shouldn't* have been so quick to judge the situation, or you. I'm sorry."

A smile played on the edge of his lips. "*Aó*, okay."

"Okay? Just *okay?* You know, this isn't easy . . ."

"I'm sure not."

Carolyn felt herself getting agitated. "Especially with . . . "

"You," they completed in harmony. Carolyn laughed, and Jesse broke into a wide smile.

"You don't make it easy to say 'I'm sorry.'"

He shrugged. "No need. There's no word in the Navajo language for 'I'm sorry.' If you're truly sorry for something, you just don't do it again."

The dog without a name stood next to Carolyn, stretched its head upward, and licked at her fingers. As she moved her hand to pet him, he bowed his head, making the backs of his ears available to her fingers.

134

Changing the subject, Carolyn looked over at Jesse as he sat down on the porch steps. "I have a question I'd like to ask you . . ."

Jesse glanced up at her. "Fire away."

"Yesterday you asked me something. You asked me what I knew about skinwalkers. Why?"

Jesse pushed a mound of sand with the toe of his boot, studying it soberly. After a long pause, he said, "Just curious."

"I don't think so." She sat down next to him and watched a lizard pad toward them across the sand; its splayed feet lifted and fell like little pistons. When it saw them, it stopped and stared, eyes unblinking, a vein beating visibly in its neck. Then it skittered behind a clump of rocks. The dog ran after it, nosing through the rocks and weeds in excited circles, searching in vain for the vanished critter.

"Yesterday wasn't my first encounter with a skinwalker," Carolyn confided. "Apparently, it was at my window the night my horse disappeared. I wondered if I had dreamt it, or if it had been you, and my eyes had played tricks on me, you know, seeing someone hooded in a wolf's skin. But I know now that it was real, whatever it is, and it's been watching me and following me. It's scary."

Jesse rested his elbows on his knees, pressing his chin against his fists. He listened intently, occasionally nodding in affirmation. "Have you told your mom and dad?"

Carolyn shook her head. "They'd either ground me out of concern for my safety or they'd think I was making up the whole thing. Either way, it's best I keep it to myself for now. But I needed to talk to someone about it. I guess you're the lucky guy. And I need to know what you know about skinwalkers."

Another pause, but Jesse nodded slowly, choosing his words carefully. *"Yee naaldlooshii,"* he said. "That's the Navajo name for what you've seen and felt. It's a witch. An *aditlgashii.* But I don't have any idea why it would be interested in you."

Carolyn looked at him with a what-do-you-mean-by-that? stare.

"No offense. I just don't know why he would be stalking you, what the connection would be."

"Have you ever seen him?"

"No. But I've felt him, just like you have. My grandfather claims to have had several run-ins with him. He says the *yee naaldlooshii* burned down his brush arbor; he shot at it, but it disappeared. Most likely his aim was so bad that he ended up missing the wolf by a mile. Then yesterday, he told me the wolf had spoken to him one night—about a week ago. It upset him so much that he ended up in the hospital. He had a stroke."

"I'm sorry."

In the silence that followed, Carolyn sensed that Jesse was struggling with how much or how little he should divulge. Finally, he pulled a leather cord from around his neck and handed it to her; she sat down next to him and looked at it. From the middle dangled a large perforated coin. "He told me the *yee naaldlooshii* gave him coins like this one."

She inspected the coin, studied what appeared to be a shield with a lion crescent emblazoned on one side and portraits of three men wearing crowns on the other.

"Wow. It's really old, isn't it?" She could barely make out the writing but guessed it was Spanish. "Where did it come from?"

He shrugged. "All I know is that my grandfather claims the *yee naaldlooshii* is bringing them to him from the Land of the Dead. It's a long story, but my grandfather says they're the same coins he laid in his brother's coffin sixty years ago. I know it sounds crazy, and it probably is."

"How did you get this one?" she asked, appreciating that he was sharing so much with her. It must have been bothering him for a long time. She handed the necklace back to him.

"Another story. My father was a cop . . . he died about a year ago. His partner said they found this coin on him when they recovered his body from his wrecked vehicle. That's all anyone knows about it."

"Your mom just told me about the accident."

The boy tossed a stone toward the rocks where the lizard had disappeared, then straightened his shoulders. "I don't believe it was an *accident*. I believe he was *murdered*. And there seems to be some connection between this coin, my father's death, my grandfather's sickness, and the *yee naaldlooshii* who's causing both you and the old man trouble. I just don't have any idea what it is. Especially why you're involved. Somehow, for some reason, he must consider you a threat."

"Yeah, I'm a real threat, all right. How could I . . ."

Jesse shook his head. "I don't know. But you're tied in, somehow."

Carolyn accepted this as fact. "Your grandfather says he put coins like these in his brother's coffin," she said mostly to herself. "Where did he get them?"

"He won't say. Just says he stole them from Broken Bones, whoever *that* is. I know. It's crazy."

"How did his brother die?"

"My mother told me once. I think he came down with pneumonia or something."

The mutt gave up on the lizard, returned, and plopped himself down between Carolyn and Jesse. Jesse ignored him. "Who told you about skinwalkers?" he asked.

"Lena mostly, one of the women who works at the store."

He nodded. "She's my aunt."

"Really? She's nice. My dad told her how I woke up my first night at Standing Rock and thought I saw someone wearing an animal's skull staring in at me through my window. It scared the living daylights out of me. I think my parents believe I dreamt it all up, but Lena said it was a skinwalker. I didn't know what to believe, until yesterday. I felt it out there. It was following me. It spooked Nakai. To be honest, I don't know if it was spying on me or *hunting* me. Maybe it *vontid to drrink my blud*."

Jesse looked up at her and she laughed.

"A bad habit of mine. I get the heebee-jeebies anytime skinwalkers start following me around. Another character flaw."

Jesse smiled, an upward corkscrew of the lips. A dimple formed on one cheek, which Carolyn found attractive.

"You *are* a funny girl."

Not a word was spoken for a moment, and the silence bothered neither of them.

Finally Carolyn said, "Teddy."

"Hmm?" Jesse surfaced from wherever he'd been.

"His name is Teddy."

"Whose?"

"Our pal here. Doesn't he kind of look like a big teddy bear?"

Jesse shrugged.

"Since he needs a name, I've decided on Teddy. Did you see his ears prick forward? I think he likes it."

CHAPTER EIGHTEEN

If the answers don't come to you, then you must go to the answers. His father had always said that; now it was up to him to put it into practice. Jesse followed the old sheep trail toward the home of the crystal gazer. It was already getting late; the sun was low enough that shadows slanted in long stretches from every tree. Teddy followed.

Since his christening that morning, the dog had started behaving as though he now belonged to somebody. He had never followed Jesse away from the house before, preferring instead to stay beneath a tree and watch the comings and goings. It must be all the attention he received from Carolyn, Jesse figured.

Teddy. What a dumb name.

Carolyn's visit had surprised him; his feelings toward her surprised him even more. She was so bright and enthusiastic, so sincere, so funny. He was amazed how easy it was to talk to her. And, of course, her looks were flawless: the bright eyes, the sculpted cheekbones, the chiseled nose. If there was any fault in her looks at all, it was that the perfection of her features also gave her a slightly cool, distant look.

And she seemed to like him. That was surprising too. She was probably just lonely or bored, Jesse told himself. He would be careful not to read too much into this new relationship. They could be friends without him following her around, acting like Teddy.

Topping the ridge, Jesse looked down at the crystal gazer's summer hogan. Desbah Yazzie spent her winters with relatives in Chinle, then came back to Red Rock in the spring. She was one of the most respected medicine women on the reservation, specializing in finding something or someone lost, in identifying witches, and in diagnosing illnesses so that the proper ceremony could be performed. She also claimed to have retired.

Her camp consisted of two octagonal hogans built of unpeeled pine logs, a small storage shed desperately in need of repair, a tilted outhouse, and a brush arbor among a cluster of cedar trees. Past the arbor stood two sheep pens made of cedar poles, bedsprings, sections of wire fencing, and odd lengths of wooden planks, grayed from years of sunlight. Cooking utensils hung under the arbor, and clothes were hanging out to air. The ground was clean and recently raked. There weren't any dogs or other animals in sight, with the exception of Teddy. A stillness lay over the camp like an enchanted sleep.

Jesse tied his horse to a gnarled piñon and approached the nearest hogan. Smoke drifted upward in lazy spirals from the stovepipe that pierced the earth-covered roof. He waited near the door which eventually grated open. A voice like a rusty nail croaked out at him. *"Yá'át'ééh,* Twilight Boy. I've been expecting you. Come in. Come in."

Jesse blinked, unsure now if he wanted to or not. He hadn't seen Desbah Yazzie in years, the last time

141

being at a squaw dance in Window Rock. She hadn't changed any. Skinny as a fencepost, she was dressed in the traditional layers of skirts and a blue velvet blouse. Her thin gray hair was gathered back into the customary bun, wrapped with heavy wool string.

The woman's most distinguishing trait was the reflective sunglasses she always wore, even at night. They say it hid her blindness. Jesse didn't know if she was fully blind or not; every time he had seen her, she seemed to get around okay. She didn't carry a cane, at least he'd never seen her with one, nor did she move with the hesitancy you'd expect from a blind person.

When Jesse stepped inside, he could barely make out her movement among the evening shadows. Desbah Yazzie maneuvered easily through the darkness of her home, gathering items, stowing them in a pillowcase. "You can wait there by the door, boy," she said in Navajo. "Let me get a few things before we go to the other hogan. That's where I do my work."

A moment later, he followed her outside and around back to the smaller hogan, where Desbah fumbled with the lock and key. She pushed the door open and disappeared inside. The air that greeted him at the entrance was cool and smelled of earth; inside it was pitch black. The crystal gazer called him to follow.

Jesse stooped to clear the door frame and then walked clockwise around the perimeter, repeating the pathway of the sun. This he had learned from his parents at a ceremony years ago. The waning sun outside provided just enough light for him to see Desbah Yazzie seated in the center of the dirt floor of the empty room, a Navajo blanket spread in front of her. Unsure of what to do, Jesse sat down across from her and waited, watching the reflections off her mirrored lenses.

"This morning I told the Earth and Sky you were coming," she said to him. "I said, 'You are welcome, Twilight Boy, and I will arrange things for our meeting. I want to reflect you, the Sky, and you, the Earth. You open the secrets. I will simply arrange things.'"

"How do you know my warrior name?" Jesse asked. The question resulted in a toothless smile from the medicine woman, but no answer.

When he was eight years old, Jesse had been initiated by the *Yeibichei,* the holy dancers, at a Night Way ceremony. The secret name they had given him was Twilight Boy. They told him this was his name because he had been born in Flagstaff, Arizona, beneath *Dook'o'oosliid,* the Sacred Mountain of the West, the mountain where the Twilight Boy of Navajo mythology was placed amid the sunbeams and black clouds to dwell with Talking God. His mother had buried his umbilical cord there, tying Jesse forever to the Sacred Mountain and to Diné Bakiyah, Land of the People.

"Why would you come see me if I couldn't tell you things you'd be surprised I know?" she asked. She opened her medicine bundle, setting a slab of crystal on the blanket next to her. Then she dug into the pillow case and pulled out her *jish* bag of sacred things and laid them out: prayer sticks, the stone fetish of a bear, a leather pouch containing arrowheads and pieces of shell.

Jesse watched without saying a word. When she had everything arranged as she wanted, she inquired about his mother, his grandfather's health, the simple pleasantries any doctor might extend. He told her his mother was fine, that her grieving over his father had become less, that she would even laugh on rare occasions now. He told her about his grandfather's stroke, unsure if she knew about it or not, and about the skinwalker, the little his grandfather had shared with him. The mention of the *Yee naaldlooshii* led to the reason he was here: to learn what he could about the mysterious coins, to find out anything possible about his father's accident. Jesse handed her his coin necklace, and she closed her thin fingers around the gold for a long moment. She then placed it next to the other items on her blanket. He finished his story by telling her about his visit with the *bilagáana* girl, and her tale about being stalked by the *Yee naaldlooshii*.

Desbah Yazzie sat in silence, carefully tearing a page of newspaper into tiny pieces and dropping the flakes into a charred coffee can. Next she shredded a piece of cloth into thin strips and added it to the pot.

"It is right that you came to see me, Twilight Boy." She turned her face toward him. "There are forces at work here that are not in harmony. There is witchcraft at your doorstep."

"What can I do?"

"You must have harmony. *Hózhóni*. It is the Blessing Way. It is Walking in Beauty."

"How do I walk in beauty?" he asked. He had heard the phrase many times before, but it had always seemed so vague.

The crystal gazer shook her head. "Our children

144

are losing touch with the old ways; it is unfortunate. To Walk in Beauty is to be obedient. Obedience is law. It is doing things in the right way at the right time. It is order, like spring before summer, autumn before winter. It is harmony, the pleasing combination of Man and Mother Earth. It is respect for nature; it is being in accord with the universe. You must respect yourself, and you must live in order with the sun, moon, and stars."

The old woman pulled out a plastic prescription bottle from her *jish* bag and twisted off the cap. She sprinkled a pinch of corn pollen from it onto the crystal, then began chanting a blessing song.

Jesse sat with his head bowed, his hands open, palms turned upward. He heard the striking of a match and looked up as Desbah dropped the flame into the coffee can. A moment later, fire licked the edges of the can, casting a soft glow across the room. The medicine woman's shadow danced against the walls, hovering like black ghosts on the hogan's walls. She picked up the crystal and held it to the fire; its light reflected off her glasses, off the translucent stone.

"Ah," she breathed. "Here it is . . . the prism of the cosmos revealed. The windows of the past are open. The door to the future stands ajar.

"I see treachery. I see bags of golden coins strewn across the rocks, sprinkled amongst the bones of men. I see greed and lust licking at the bones in the form of a wolf, a man wolf. The *Yee naaldlooshii.*

"I see an old man . . . your grandfather. He's sick with whiskey, plagued by *chindi.* He has your answers, yet they are buried so deep in his grief you will never find them, not from him. I see a girl . . . lithe as a young fawn, as pretty as a dewdrop. She's a danger to you . . .

"And I see the past . . . I see a boy of your age—your grandfather—he is homesick and decides to run away from boarding school and rejoin his family. It is late autumn; the cottonwoods are already bare skeletons and the wild grass is yellowed by frost. Chee plans to slip out of the dormitory late at night, make a twenty-mile hike in the dark, and be home before anyone realizes he is missing.

"His younger brother Tyrone pleads to go with him, but Chee insists that he stay. The nights are bitter cold, and Chee knows the journey will be dangerous. Tyrone persists, and Chee gives in."

Desbah Yazzie cocked her head sideways for a moment as though she were listening to something, then continued: "As Chee feared, the night trek becomes too difficult for his little brother; Tyrone slows their pace considerably. The trail is steep and treacherous terrain. Chee threatens to leave his brother behind, tiring of the boy's complaints about the cold and their grueling pace. By morning they have covered only half the distance that Chee originally intended. He knows the B.I.A. truant officers will soon be searching for them.

"It begins to snow. The boys have no extra clothing, no matches, just the small amount of food that Chee had collected from his supper plate the day before. Their feet are frostbitten. By sunrise, snow has covered the ground, making it impossible to know if they are still on the trail that leads over Waterless Mesa and *Tseh ii aha,* Red Butte. The fear of getting lost quickly replaces any worries of being apprehended by truant officers. They hike on, plodding through the heavy snow.

"It is around noon when they finally spot an outcropping of rock that is deep enough to offer shelter. The two boys go inside the grotto and become the unsuspecting guests of the Devil."

The crystal gazer's voice dropped to a whisper: "I see Coins from the Dead. There are bags of them, a fortune. Coins spilled across the body of the broken skeleton of a man, a conquistador by the looks of the helmet lying nearby. An arrow shaft is embedded in his ribcage."

Broken Bones. Jesse recalled his grandfather's reference to the coins belonging to "Broken Bones."

"The two boys stare at their discovery in terror," Desbah Yazzie uttered in a soft, distant voice. "They realize they have contaminated themselves in a lair of *chindi*. A ceremony to purify them of the ghost sickness would have to be given.

"But greed is greed, is it not? Chee rationalizes that since a curing ceremony is in order anyway, why not help themselves to a handful of the coins? Maybe they could come back later with their father and have the entire area cleansed, take the bags of gold, and live happily, never having to go back to school again. Such are the thoughts of young boys.

"Tyrone is more hesitant, fearful of even touching the coins. But at his older brother's insistence, he too delves into the broken bags of coins. By the time they finally make it home that afternoon, the truant officers are there waiting for them. The boys, half frozen and exhausted, are driven back to their dorm that evening.

147

They have had no time to share their discovery with family, let alone go through the rites of a curing ceremony. Chee swears Tyrone to secrecy, hoping to return to their find in the summer. Unfortunately, Tyrone dies that spring.

"Chee blames himself, of course, believing ghost sickness caused his brother's death. It had been his idea to loot the treasure of the dead, so he considers himself ultimately responsible for what has happened. Chee figures his life is spared only to be tormented with guilt, a burden he will carry to his grave."

"How do these coins keep showing up?" Jesse asked. "My grandfather told me that he buried them with Tyrone in an effort to give them back to the Dead."

A gust of wind blew down the smokehole into the hogan, fanning the flame in the can for just a moment before putting it out. Ashes and smoke drifted upward, silvery confetti.

The crystal gazer set down her stone and stared motionlessly out the doorway. It had once again become still.

"You must beware, Twilight Boy," she said, again turning her mirrored eyes toward him. "The dark powers you seek to expose are very strong. The *Yee naaldlooshii* is aware of your danger to him, and he will stop at nothing to protect his interests. What he desires is close at hand, and only you stand in his way."

"How do I stand in his way?"

"You seek to expose him. And you are right to do so. It was the *Yee naaldlooshii* who caused your father's death."

"How?"

148

The crystal gazer shook her head. "I don't know. It is too well hidden. As I said, he has powers of his own. It was his dark wind that has smothered the flame. To expose a skinwalker invariably means its death. This is all I can tell you."

She gathered her items and stuffed them back inside the pillowcase, handing Jesse his coin. It was now completely dark outside, making it impossible to see more than her thin silhouette. When she stood to leave, Jesse followed.

"Do you smoke, Twilight Boy?"

Jesse looked at her, dumbfounded.

"Do you smoke?" she asked again.

"No."

"That's good," she said. "But unfortunately, this old woman does."

Jesse didn't say anything.

"Do me a favor, would you, young man? Pick me up a carton of cigarettes. It's difficult for me to get into town these days, or even to the trading post. I have plenty of food, my niece sees to that, but she refuses to support my harmful pleasures."

Jesse nodded.

"Remember, a whole carton."

Again he nodded. Small payment for the services of a crystal gazer.

CHAPTER NINETEEN

That night the old woman looked through her darkness toward Waterless Mesa. Just eight miles south as the crow flies lay all that gold. If a person were to comb the area . . . She smiled to herself, amused by her own foolishness. It was blood money. Men had already died for it; their *chindi* contaminated the coins like flies on spoiled meat.

Unfortunately, others still might die for it. The wolf was on the prowl.

Desbah Yazzie's hands, twisted with age and arthritis, reached up and removed her sunglasses. Her sight had been taken long ago, but the Calling Gods spoke to her, giving her new vision.

Her sightless eyes were now exposed to the soft moonlight. She turned southward, allowed the night breeze to cool the tired white orbs. Somewhere a coyote howled, its call sounding like the cry of a small child.

CHAPTER TWENTY

It was a hot Monday afternoon, three days since Jesse had been to see Desbah Yazzie. The cowbell above the door clanged as he entered Red Rock Trading Post. The crystal gazer had warned him away from Carolyn, had made it clear that she was somehow a danger to him. But how could she be? Carolyn was on his side, he was sure of that. And if she was a danger to him, then he would just have to deal with that along with everything else.

He had borrowed the truck today to visit his grandfather, and the old man had dropped another bombshell in his lap. He had to tell Carolyn.

"You're an hour early." His mother smiled up at him as she stamped tags on cans of soup with something that looked like a cross between a handgun and paper stapler.

"I know. I have to talk to Carolyn about something."

"Just don't forget that I get off in an hour. If I can't find you, I'll leave without you." She held out her hand: "Keys."

Jesse handed them to her, returning her grin. "I'm driving."

"If you're here," she replied. "Remember, one hour."

Jesse nodded and set off looking for Carolyn. He

hoped she was here at the store and he wouldn't have to go over to her house. That would be awkward.

He passed Carolyn's dad, hunched over the counter, shuffling through a stack of papers. Mr. Manchester tucked a pen behind his ear and glanced up through owlish glasses; concentration furrowed his brow. It took a moment for recognition to set in, then he acknowledged Jesse with a nod. "How's it going?" he said.

"Fine." Jesse wondered if Mr. Manchester was thinking about the day he and Carolyn had come by to retrieve their horse.

"Can I help you with something?"

Jesse had never asked to see someone's daughter before. "Uhm . . . yeah. Can I have a carton of cigarettes?"

Mr. Manchester gave him a sharp look, then turned around and procured a red and white carton from the shelf. "Fourteen ninety-five," he said, tossing it on the counter. "And I'll need to see some I.D."

Not this ID business again. Jesse pulled a twenty out of his pocket and realized what a dumb thing he'd just done. *A great way to impress a girl's dad, all right. What an idiot. The reputed horse thief and Peeping Tom is also a chain-smoker.*

"I don't have any."

Mr. Manchester slid the carton away. "Sorry. I don't sell cigarettes to minors."

"They're not for me," Jesse fumbled. "Desbah Yazzie asked me to get them for her. It's my payment."

"Who?"

"The local shaman," Jesse heard someone behind him say. He turned to see Harlan Mitchell approaching

152

the counter. "Or should I say *loco* shaman?" Jesse started to speak but was again interrupted.

"It's unfortunate so many of my people waste their time and money on soothsayers and quacks. Superstition is one of the major weaknesses of the Diné."

Mr. Manchester dipped into the cash register and handed Jesse his change. "I'll sell them to you this once, son, but next time you'll have to have a note from your mother." Jesse promised himself there wouldn't be a next time.

Harlan looked at him and his eyes softened. "So how's the old woman doing these days? I haven't seen her in years."

"She's fine," Jesse replied tightly.

"Pardon me for speaking out of turn. One of the peculiarities of being an old man is just how often you find opportunities to be opinionated. Give the woman my regards."

"How's the painting coming?" Mr. Manchester asked Harlan.

"The first coat is finished. But we're going to have to run into Gallup to pick up more paint."

"Sounds good. Take the pickup. We've got an open account with Gallup Lumber." Harlan nodded and headed toward the back door. Mr. Manchester smiled at Jesse as he bagged the carton of cigarettes.

"There you are, son. Remember, just get a note from your mom next time. It will save a lot of hassle."

Hassle is right. Peering down the aisle, he noticed Carolyn watching him from one of the other cash registers. He remembered to thank Mr. Manchester before heading her way. Dressed in shorts and a light cotton blouse with her hair pulled back into a pony tail, she looked great. She smiled as he approached, shaking her head.

"What kind of trouble did you get into now?"

He grinned back at her, holding up the transparent plastic bag. She took in its contents and raised her eyebrows. Jesse continued grinning, finding it impossible to wipe the foolish expression off his face.

"My dad calls them cancer sticks," Carolyn remarked with a trace of admonition in her voice.

"We Navajos call them cigarettes," Jesse chided. "Lighten up. They're not for me."

Carolyn pushed her glasses back in place. "Did you tell my father that?"

"I started to, until the lecture began on how superstitions have kept us Navajos living in the Dark Ages."

"Harlan?"

Jesse nodded.

"I think Harlan Mitchell missed his calling," Carolyn said. "He should've been a professor or something. Don't you think?"

Jesse shrugged. "I guess. Anyway, I've got some interesting news to tell you. I went to see a crystal gazer, and I had another talk with my grandfather."

"Hold on. Let me get someone to cover the register . . ." Carolyn waved at Lena Tsosie, who was cleaning windows at the front of the store. "Lena, could you take over for me for a little while. I've got to take care of something."

Lena inspected her reflection in the glass, then waved

back in their direction. "Go ahead. I'll be right there."

Stepping outside, Carolyn directed Jesse toward a large cottonwood. "Okay. What's your news?" she said, casting a glance over her shoulder. But Jesse wasn't behind her. She turned and saw him crouched near the steps in front of the store, examining something on the ground. Two young girls maneuvered around him as they pranced up the steps ahead of their mother.

"What is it?" Carolyn asked, moving back to Jesse. He looked up at her, a strange look on his face.

"Look here."

She stared at the trampled ground where he was pointing, noticed a large red ant carrying something up and down hills and valleys. She shrugged, *So what?*

"Do you see this track?"

Carolyn nodded.

"See the rounded toe, the flat heel?"

Again she nodded, a little more impatient this time. *Okay. Cut to the chase.*

Jesse's middle finger traced along a fine line of raised earth near the center of the shoe print. "Do you see this?"

She squatted down near him, her interest finally piqued. The herculean ant veered off at a ninety-degree angle, bearing its freight toward the wilderness of sand dunes and badlands that made up the parking lot. "Okay?" The inflection in her voice made her reply a question.

Jesse's eyes narrowed. "This is the same track that I found near my grandfather's hogan after the fire. It belongs to the *Yee naaldlooshii.*"

Jesse's revelation refused to connect in Carolyn's thoughts. "How can you be so sure? It's just one faded print in the ground, one among a hundred or more."

Jesse's look said he was sure. He stood up slowly, scanned the ground for other signs. Several feet away from the steps, the telltale earth became less hard packed, an ant's nightmare of windblown sand. It would be impossible to track any prints in that quagmire of loose dirt. Convinced that there were no more signs of the boot print, Jesse finally allowed Carolyn to lead the way over to the shade of the cottonwood. They sat there, Jesse silent and brooding. Teddy appeared from a shaded alcove and joined them, wagging his tail and plopping down next to Carolyn.

"So he's been at the store," she said, scratching the mongrel behind the ears. It was an obvious deduction, needing no confirmation. But the implication was horrific. The simple fact that this *thing*, this skinwalker, could masquerade as something human and fraternize with the unaware . . . it unnerved her. She wanted to discredit Jesse's find, but his stern expression made her reluctant to try.

Eventually, Jesse was able to tell her about his visit with Desbah Yazzie, explaining a medicine woman's role in the Navajo community. He told Carolyn what the shaman had seen in her crystal, careful to omit the part about Carolyn being a danger to him. She listened intently, occasionally interjecting an idea or asking a question.

"So there's actually a Spanish treasure out there somewhere," she said when he finished.

Jesse nodded. "Yeah."

"Did she tell you exactly where it was?"

"Nope. She just said there were bags of gold coins scattered across the rocks. My grandfather found them a long time ago. They were lying next to a skeleton. That's where he gets the notion of returning them to Broken Bones. The coins keep popping up even though he buried them with his younger brother Tyrone years ago. The *Yee naaldlooshii* has them."

"Why did your grandfather bury the coins in the first place?" Carolyn asked, not wanting to think too much about the witch. "Why didn't he just keep the money?"

"Navajo belief. You see, we stay away from the dead. We believe the *chindi* remains after a person dies, and will cause sickness or death to anyone who bothers the dwellings of the dead."

"What are *chindi?*"

"Spirits," Jesse replied. "Evil spirits. When a person dies, all that was good about him leaves this world. Only the other part remains."

"Do you believe that?"

Jesse shrugged, tossing a pebble at an imaginary target. "My grandfather told me he must return his coins to the dead. That would be his reason for doing so, to ward off evil."

"So what do we do now?" Carolyn asked, moving farther beneath the trees for shade. A crow fluttered amid the branches, causing a ruckus.

"This is where it gets good," said Jesse, emphatically. "I told you, I was out to see my grandfather this morning . . . well, I was able to get him to talk a little more about the skinwalker. He told me that the *Yee naaldlooshii* warned him that he would return in a fortnight, on the Dark Night, the night with no moon. The skinwalker said he would accompany my grandfather to where the *chindi* cry out for their gold. He said that after the coins were returned to the dead, he would never bother my grandfather again."

"Do you believe him?"

"Who?"

"Your grandfather. Do you believe the skinwalker actually told him that? Maybe he dreamt it, or maybe . . ."

"Maybe what? Maybe he's nuts?"

"I didn't say that."

"But the thought did cross your mind. And mine too. With all the booze he drinks, he could've made it all up."

"But if he didn't . . ."

"If he didn't," Jesse said, tossing another stone, "then we need to find out when the next night without a moon happens to fall. Since it's already been close to two weeks since the warning, the time must be near. We'll have to be there, waiting for the skinwalker to show up."

"And do what? Jump out of the bushes and yell 'Surprise?'"

"Something like that," Jesse said, looking up at her with cold, serious eyes. "We'll have to expose him. If we can, he'll die."

"Oh, I get it," Carolyn replied, feeling more and more apprehensive about all this madness. "We jump out of the bushes, yell 'Surprise!' The skinwalker dies, and we live happily ever after."

Jesse couldn't help but smile. "Yeah, we could do it that way, or we could trap him."

"How?"

He shrugged his shoulders. "I'm not sure. It will be more difficult than trapping someone human. A *Yee naaldlooshii* can turn into a wolf, or an owl, or even a ghost bird. But I do have a .22."

"Oh, great! My hero here will take on a skinwalker with a .22. Don't you need a silver bullet or something? This is getting more bizarre by the minute. I'm beginning to think you're really nuts."

They both laughed. Carolyn waited for the moment to pass, then pressed her shoe against Jesse's. "I can't help but wonder why a skinwalker would be so interested in having your grandfather return his coins to the dead. Why would he care?"

"Maybe he's in league with the dead," Jesse offered. "Maybe the dead speak to him."

Carolyn shook her head, the skeptical side of her unwilling to accept this. "Or maybe the skinwalker himself is trying to get the gold and needs your grandfather's help. Instead of being interested in returning the gold, maybe he's after the treasure himself."

"You're forgetting that it's the skinwalker who's been returning the coins to my grandfather in the first place. Seems he already has the gold in his possession."

"Not all of it," Carolyn reminded him. "Remember, you told me that the skinwalker was returning the coins that Chee had placed in his brother's coffin. If they are actually the same coins, that would mean that the skinwalker only has a small portion of the treasure. It seems that your grandfather is the only person living who knows where this treasure is hidden. The crystal gazer said there were bags of gold hidden out there somewhere, right?"

Jesse nodded. It made sense, he guessed. As much sense as any of this did. Carolyn's idea certainly provided a motive behind the *Yee naaldlooshii's* acts of terror. But if the *Yee naaldlooshii* already knew so much about the gold, why plague the old man? Why involve Chee if the only thing the skinwalker wanted was the gold? If he had the power to resurrect the gold that was buried with Tyrone, wouldn't he also know where the rest of the gold was hidden?

"There's something else I need to tell you," Carolyn said, her eyes watching him soberly. She didn't move her foot away. Jesse looked over at her, waiting for what he was sure would be more unexplainable pieces to their puzzle.

"When I was out at your place, I didn't tell you about something else that's been bothering me . . . or I should say *someone* else. One of my dad's employees, Tullie. Do you know him?"

Jesse nodded. "Kind of." An image of a slow-footed, lumbering giant came to mind.

"Last week, after you came to my rescue, I had another strange thing happen to me that same day. When I went over to the store, I saw Tullie there, soaking wet. When I said something to him, he acted like he wanted to strangle me. He's scary. My dad said he was putting up fenceposts and he got caught in the rain. I don't buy it . . . I think he was out there, following me. You should've seen the way he glared at me when I said something about him being all dirty and wet. I told him he was making a mess of my dad's floor."

"I'm sure he appreciated you correcting him."

"It's more than that. And it isn't the first time I've noticed him sort of hanging around on the sidelines, staring at me like I was something he wanted to peel off his shoes. It's creepy."

"Maybe we need to do a little investigating of Tullie," Jesse said. "See where he lives, find out about his past. I could ask around."

"I already have. I've learned that he's all alone, and no one really knows much more about him. That's what my dad told me, anyway."

"Interesting. I'll see if my grandfather knows him, see if there's any connection."

Weary of the topic, Carolyn grabbed Jesse's hand and pulled him up with her. "Come on. I want you to meet my mom."

"That's okay."

"Come on," she coaxed, yanking his arm. "You'll like her." Jesse reluctantly followed, enjoying holding Carolyn's hand. Her palm was cool and soft, her fingers strong. Teddy watched as they walked toward the cottage, reluctant to give up his shade. When they entered the house, Carolyn casually dropped Jesse's hand and yelled, "Mom!"

"In here!" a voice called back. Her mother was in the living room, kneeling near the far wall, a tape measure in hand. She looked up and smiled.

"Hi. What's up?" Carolyn asked.

"I'm measuring the room for carpeting. I was thinking of going with either a mauve or a sandy beige. What do you think?"

"Definitely mauve."

Her mother stood and held out her hand. "Hi. I'm Beverly. You must be Jesse."

Jesse nodded, shaking her hand. "Hi," he managed.

"It's nice to meet you," Mrs. Manchester continued. "Carolyn has mentioned you quite often lately."

Jesse glanced over at Carolyn who was standing a few feet away. It could have been miles.

"She says you're quite the artist. I'd love to see your work some time."

Jesse stood there, nodding like an imbecile. He could have told her there were several of his sculptures at the trading post already, waiting to be sold on consignment, but he didn't.

"She also told me about the coin you have," she said, undaunted by the one-sided conversation, "the one that was your father's. I'd be interested in seeing it sometime, if you wouldn't mind."

Carolyn nudged him, and somewhat reluctantly, Jesse pulled off his necklace and surrendered it to Carolyn's mother. He wondered what else Carolyn had told her as he watched the woman study the coin. He noticed that she had the same intent expression he had seen in the daughter.

"Unbelievable," she said. "Hold on, I'll be right back . . ."

Carolyn winked at him as her mother hurried off.

"My mom loves doing this kind of stuff. You can imagine all the help I get on school reports. It comes in handy having an author for a mom." Her mother returned with a book as thick as a dictionary. *The Encyclopedia of Coins* was imprinted in gold on the cover. She riffled through the pages.

"I've been a coin collector for years, as Carolyn may have told you. I'm sure this coin is Spanish, but I've never seen one this old . . . Okay, here we are."

Both Carolyn and Jesse leaned over the book. Carolyn's mother pointed to a photograph of a coin exactly like Jesse's.

"It says here that it's a Spanish ducat, minted in the early sixteenth century. The three portraits are of Maximilian I and his grandsons, Charles V and Ferdinand I. See this—on the other side is a coat of arms displaying the towers of Castile and the Lions of Leon."

"Wow," Carolyn interpolated. "Where did it come from?"

Her mom looked up at her with the expression that always made Carolyn feel like she had said something really stupid. "Spain."

"I know that. I mean, I wonder how Jesse's father ended up with it."

Her mother shrugged. "My guess is that someone found it lying around out here and Jesse's father either bought it or someone gave it to him. It was probably his good-luck piece."

Real good luck, Carolyn thought. But what her mother said made sense. More sense than Jesse's idea that the coin was somehow related to his father's accident.

But it was strange that Jesse's dad had never shown it to his wife or son. And strange too was the fact that Jesse's grandfather was getting these coins dropped off at his doorstep in the middle of the night.

"Interesting, though, that ol' Francisco lost a few ducats along the way," her mother said. Carolyn must have looked confused.

"Francisco Coronado, the explorer," her mother explained. "His conquistadors came through here around 1540, I believe. It's exciting this came up: I've just been doing research on it for my novel. They traveled through here on their way to Cíbola. Their expedition was financed quite lavishly by Spain. I imagine the soldiers had plenty of pocket change for gambling and little else to do with their money. So who knows? It's possible this coin actually belonged to one of Coronado's men. Or, since this entire region was under the rule of Spain for a couple of centuries, the coin could have been dropped by any merchant, monk, soldier, or tax collector. Either way, it's quite a find. I'm sure the curator over at the museum at El Morro would be interested in seeing it."

"El what?" Carolyn asked.

"El Morro," Jesse answered.

"What's that?"

"A bluff about twenty miles from here," her mother explained. "It's also known as Inscription Rock. It's a national monument. For over three hundred years, Spanish soldiers and priests journeyed between Santa Fe and Zuni, passing El Morro on their way. Many of the travelers carved their names and other notations into the soft sandstone. It's an interesting place to

164

visit—we'll have to take you there sometime. Your father and I visited it on our first trip through here."

"Have you ever been there?" Carolyn asked Jesse.

"Once. On a school field trip in fourth grade. It's a cool place. I remember there's a lot of stuff written all over the rock, most of it in Spanish, though, so I wasn't able to read it. There's also some old Indian pictures carved in the rock."

Mrs. Manchester nodded. "That's right. There's a pool there, fed by rainwater. It's attracted people for centuries. I could read you a dozen names of Spaniards who traveled the route, so it's really not that surprising that a Spanish ducat would be found around here."

Jesse glanced over at Carolyn and their eyes met for a second, long enough to agree that now was not the time to share what they had learned from the crystal gazer.

Carolyn's mother was a walking encyclopedia. She told them more about El Morro and the role Spain played in shaping the culture of the Southwest. Finally, Carolyn remembered that she hadn't fed Nakai, and their conspirators' huddle broke up. Mrs. Manchester returned the coin necklace and again said how pleased she was to meet Jesse. He managed to stammer a thank you and a nice-to-meet-you-too.

He was glad to be outside and said so. Carolyn laughed. Jesse suddenly remembered the rendezvous he was supposed to keep with his mother and glanced at his watch. He was already ten minutes late.

"I forgot. Mom's waiting—I've gotta go."

Carolyn watched him jog toward the store. Teddy was nowhere in sight. "When should we go to the library?" she shouted after him.

"Library?" he asked, walking backward.

"We need to find a lunar calendar."

He nodded. They needed to find out when the next night without a moon occurred — the Dark Night. Time was running out, and there was still a wolf to trap. "Soon," he answered. "Maybe tomorrow."

CHAPTER TWENTY-ONE

At the cusp of night the wolf went hunting.

Clouds concealed the moon, but a million stars shined down like heavenly eyes, watching. Watching. Eyes too far away to blink warning to an unsuspecting young pup and his mother. The wolf went hunting.

He would kill Twilight Boy tonight, and the threat would vanish. He would kill the blind hag, too, if she kept meddling in his business. Death went hunting. He slid through the black trees in silent, fluid motion.

The clouds parted and moonlight beamed downward. An owl's soft call followed him as he crept past the junk heap on four wheels and approached the trailer. A dog appeared out of nowhere, growled uncertainly. The wolf glowered at the animal, willing it to go away.

With inhuman strength he pulled himself up onto the thin aluminum roof and crawled over to the small pipe that protruded from the center of the trailer. A single, almost inaudible creak gave warning of the danger, but it fell on deaf ears.

A brief flash produced a tiny flame, which instantly disappeared, swallowed by the dark hole, the open mouth to Twilight Boy. The wolf jumped down from the roof and hid beneath the shelter of a juniper. Wisps of smoke seeped out of a window; light from the flame illuminated the interior.

The wolf drew his knife and waited. If anyone ran out, he would spill their blood on the sand. The fire grew larger, the smoke thicker, deadlier. Excitement stirred in his breast. Flames licked at the edges of curtains and then crawled up the wall. The night grew brighter.

Sparks shot upward in an explosion of glowing embers. The fire intensified. Sound exploded through the silence. Death went hunting and found its prey. As the heat intensified, the wolf backed away from the carnage; he was finished here. Lifting his knife toward the heavens, a thrill surged through him, and his triumphant scream escaped into the night.

CHAPTER TWENTY-TWO

Carolyn jerked upright, her eyes opening wide as the sound of a scream echoed in her head.

The wolf.

She had heard it. Something terrible had happened.

But that was crazy; surely it had been a dream, or something else—a dog barking or a cat's cry in the night.

She felt perspiration cool on the back of her neck; her heart raced. Disoriented, she peered out her window. Silence. No barking dog. No cat. But she knew she hadn't been dreaming, no more than she had been dreaming the night the skinwalker appeared at her window.

Jesse was in trouble.

She slipped out of bed, pulled on her robe, and left her room with the door slightly ajar so that the click of the latch wouldn't awaken her parents. In the kitchen, she snapped on the light and glanced at the clock above the range: twelve-thirty. Padding over to the refrigerator, Carolyn poured herself a glass of orange juice and sat down at the dining room table.

What should she do? Again she wished Jesse had a phone. Should she awaken her parents? Should she saddle Nakai and quietly slip out?

One thing for certain: She would dress and go to Jesse.

CHAPTER TWENTY-THREE

As if a phone could grant wishes, it suddenly rang. Carolyn, now fully clothed, dashed toward the ominous sound. As she picked up the receiver, she glanced down the hallway at her parents' bedroom door, noticed the light beneath it. "Hello?"

"Carolyn?" It was Jesse's voice.

"Yeah. Jesse? Where are you?"

"At the police station. There's been an accident."

"What happened?" Her parents were now standing near her, looking concerned but unfocused with sleep.

"There's been a fire," Jesse replied, his voice sounding shaky. "Our house—the whole thing burned down."

"Oh, my God. How?"

"What's happened?" her father asked.

"Jesse's house, it burned down tonight."

"Oh heavens," her mother gasped. "Is everyone all right?"

"Is everyone all right?" Carolyn parroted, shaking her head in disbelief.

"Yeah. We're both fine, I guess."

"How did you . . ."

"We weren't there. Luckily, the crystal gazer warned

us not to go home last night. She was standing in the road on our way home, and she told us our lives were in danger, that we weren't to step foot on our property. So we spent the night at my grandfather's.

"The police came by and picked us up about an hour ago. They drove over to my grandfather's to see if he knew where we were, since they didn't find any bodies after they put out the fire. I think Clah was surprised when he saw that Mom and I were there. Anyway, I was hoping you might come down to the station. My mom's really upset."

"Of course." Carolyn put her hand over the receiver. "Dad, can you drive me over to the police station?"

Her father nodded. "Which one, Gallup or Ramah?"

"Which one?" Carolyn repeated over the phone.

"Ramah."

"We'll be right there."

"Thanks."

The phone clicked, and Carolyn listened to the dull buzz for a moment, trying to piece together what had happened. The fire. Jesse's narrow escape. The scream of the wolf that had awakened her earlier.

"We'll get dressed," her father said, noticing for the first time that Carolyn was already fully clothed. "Why are you dressed, by the way?"

"A premonition," she explained. "I knew something terrible had happened."

Her father's brow furrowed, and her mother was about to say something.

"Hurry, you guys!" Carolyn cried. "Let's go!"

Thirty minutes later they entered the Navajo police

station at Ramah. The small building hummed with activity: Phones were ringing, police officers and fire-fighters congregated near a Coke machine. Carolyn spotted Jesse and his mom sitting across from Clah at a large, cluttered desk. She rushed over.

Jesse looked up and managed a smile. A tired smile. His eyes were red and puffy, signs that he'd been crying. Mrs. Begay looked confused and frightened. Her loose hair was unbrushed and her face was drawn.

The radio squawked as Clah turned his gaze toward Carolyn and her parents. His chair squeaked as he leaned back and steepled his fingers; he nodded coolly at Carolyn's father. Carolyn and her mother weren't acknowledged. Her father placed a hand gently on Mrs. Begay's shoulder, and her mother leaned over and gave her an awkward hug. Carolyn pulled up a chair next to her friend, smiled solemnly as tears welled up in her eyes. "I'm so sorry," she whispered.

Jesse nodded, then hunched over and studied his hands.

"How did it happen?" her father asked, glancing at Clah.

"The fire destroyed everything!" Jesse's mother sobbed.

Clah's expression said he thought that was a state-ment too obvious to need saying. "It appears to have started in the furnace room, possibly a leak in the gas line."

"The furnace room?" her mother asked. "But how? The furnace wouldn't even be on this time of year!"

"Apparently the pilot was still on, and it ignited a propane leak," Clah explained slowly, as if lecturing to a group of small children. "At least that's the fire chief's theory. We'll be investigating it further and should know more in a couple of days."

"Could it have been started on purpose?" Carolyn asked.

"Like, by a skinwalker?" Clah said, hardly concealing his cynicism. "Yeah, it's possible it could have been arson. I've heard young Mr. Begay's theory about it being the work of witchcraft, and we'll look into it; but I'm afraid we won't have any more luck finding his witch than we had finding his grandfather's. I already searched for tracks, but I didn't see any. Of course, I'll check it again in daylight."

Carolyn's parents looked at her, their expressions making it clear they wanted to know what Carolyn knew about all this. Clah looked tired. It was hard for her to believe that this man had once been Jesse's father's partner. How could he be so indifferent about another tragedy touching their lives? If a person worked closely with someone for years, wouldn't there naturally be some kind of concern for the family? Especially if that partner had died. Carolyn realized she didn't like Clah. He was too distant, too skeptical.

He watched her. His black eyes were calm but searching. She felt uncomfortable under his scrutiny and glanced at her father.

"Do you need a place to stay?" her father asked Mrs. Begay. "There's an extra room at the back of the store that could easily be made into temporary living quarters."

Jesse's mother shook her head. "No, thank you.

I'm sure we'll be able to stay at Lena's summer hogan for awhile. She's my husband's sister-in-law, so we'll be with family."

Carolyn's mother took Mrs. Begay's hand in hers. "What can we do?"

Jesse looked up at Carolyn, and their eyes locked. There was only one thing to do. It was time to hunt down a wolf.

PART IV

Black/Night

CHAPTER TWENTY-FOUR

Before opening the almanac the librarian handed her, Carolyn made her way over to a secluded corner table and reread her letter from Thomas:

Dear Carolyn,

As they say out there in the West— "Howdy."

Hope you're having a good time. Are you wearing that cowboy hat I bought you?

I'll be flying to Los Angeles on June 20th for my cousin's wedding. There's a layover in Denver, so I was able to arrange a commuter flight from there to Albuquerque. Come see me!

The time will be short—I'll get into Albuquerque at 11:50 A.M. and will have to fly out at 12:30. But it would be great to see you.

Write or call if it can't work out. If I don't hear from you before then, I'll plan on you being there. I'll arrive on Southwest Airlines, Flight 104. I'll be looking for a good-looking "gal" wearing a black Stetson.

Love, Thomas

Love, Thomas. It was just the way you ended a letter, Carolyn told herself. But it sounded right. She could hardly believe that she'd be seeing him in little more than a week!

But thinking of Thomas brought an assortment of feelings. Although she had only been on the rez for a short time, she somehow felt she wasn't the same person who left Boston a few weeks ago. And, of course, there was the question of where her relationship with Jesse was heading. Sure, she could tell herself that they were simply friends and that by the end of summer they'd both just promise to be faithful pen pals. But would it be that easy?

Thomas and Jesse. Two totally different boys. One was cool and popular, the other deep and mysterious. Two different worlds. If they ever met, would they be friends? For some reason, she doubted it.

When she first read the letter that morning, Carolyn asked her father how long a drive it would be to Albuquerque. "Less than two hours. Why?" he had said. Her next question was whether or not he'd be willing to drive her there so she could meet Thomas during his layover. Her father said that she would probably be able to talk him into it, but only after she told him what Clah meant when he said he doubted if he'd have any more luck finding Jesse's witch than he had finding his grandfather's.

Carolyn sketched out brief details about Harrison Chee's brush arbor burning down and Jesse's suspicion that his father's death was somehow connected to the coins. She still didn't think she should say anything about her own feelings of being followed the day Nakai had thrown her, or of Chee's appointed rendezvous with the skinwalker. Nor did she think her parents needed to hear about the blind crystal gazer's visions. It was best to wait on all that.

Her dad didn't prod any further, so Carolyn got off fairly easy. Her mother did caution her, however, about not getting too wrapped up in Indian superstitions. She assured Carolyn that witches could only be found in fairy tales and in costume boxes at Halloween. Carolyn nodded and kept her mouth shut for a change.

She yawned. Not much sleep last night.

After folding her letter to pocket size, she opened the almanac. It was hard to believe that it had only been twelve hours since she was sitting in the police station, staring at the bewildered faces of Jesse and his mother. She felt so sorry for them. They were supposed to spend the day sifting through what was left of their home, searching for anything worth salvaging. But Carolyn doubted if they'd been able to go—there had been a lot of rain this morning. It was needed, but the timing was terrible. Jesse and his mom would have to be wading through ashes *and* mud.

Carolyn had decided to ride into Gallup with her parents this morning and search the library for a lunar calendar. Her mom and dad had dropped her off on their way to meet their lawyer, something to do with the deed to the trading post. They promised to swing by and pick her up when they finished.

Carolyn and Jesse's plan, as far as there was a plan, was to find out when the so-called Dark Night would occur. She hadn't the slightest idea what they were going to do after they found out.

Thumbing through the almanac, she flipped to the index and looked up "Moon, the phases of," then turned to the page listed. Moon Phases: New Moon, First Quarter Moon, Full Moon, Last Quarter Moon, Moon's Perigee and Apogee . . . She turned the page. Moon Eclipses. Next page: Daily Calendar of Sunrises and Sunsets, Moon Phases, beginning with January. She flicked ahead to June, tracing a finger down the page. Following each day of the week, she observed the dark printed numbers indicating moon phases. On Friday, June 17, there were no numbers—a moonless night. The Dark Night.

June 17. That was tomorrow night!

They would have to act fast, but what could she and Jesse really do? Maybe they should just turn the information over to the police and let them deal with it. Carolyn knew they wouldn't. Remembering Clah's sarcasm and indifference just that morning, she realized that they were on their own; it was up to them to somehow reveal the witch's identity and render the skinwalker powerless. But what if it didn't work? What if the skinwalker turned on them, using his powers to silence them like he tried to do with Jesse last night? It had finally dawned on Carolyn that this wasn't merely a scary game she was playing; it was a real life-or-death situation.

She could back out, she told herself. She could turn her back on it, refuse to believe there were such things as skinwalkers and crystal gazers. She could refuse to get involved any further. But then she thought of Jesse sitting there in the police station at three in the morning, trying not to cry, trying to be brave, and his mother picking through the charred pieces of their lives. When she thought about the thing that had followed her and Nakai, slithering through the shadows, or the face staring in at her from her window . . . No, she wouldn't back out. They had to destroy it. They *could* do it.

As Carolyn pushed back her chair and stood up to return the almanac, she felt a chill.

Someone was watching her.

She turned around, scanning the quiet room, the clusters of tables, the people silently poring over books and newspapers. Her eyes moved back to the room's edges. There, in a shadowed area, a man casually pulled a book off a shelf and thumbed through it, pretending to be absorbed. She stared at him, adjusting her glasses with an index finger. He looked familiar, but she couldn't place him . . . Finally, he looked up from his book, glanced over at her, and, with a slight smile, nodded.

It was Clah. Carolyn hadn't recognized him out of uniform. He was dressed in faded jeans, black engineer boots, and a black leather jacket. A red bandanna crossed his forehead and was knotted against his short-cropped hair.

He walked toward her.

Carolyn's heart seemed to stop. but she knew it was important that she appear calm. She nodded back, waiting for him to approach.

"A perfect day for browsing through books," Clah greeted her.

Carolyn didn't say anything.

"May I?"

She handed him the almanac.

"Hmm. Interesting reading material. Lots of valuable

information in here, isn't there? But not what I'd expect a young girl to find interesting. I'd have expected you to be reading young romance novels or fashion magazines." He made no attempt to disguise his sarcasm.

"It's interesting," Carolyn stammered, reaching defensively for the book.

Clah held onto it a moment before allowing her to have it back. His smile vanished. "I'm sure. But sometimes too much research can be hazardous to one's health, don't you think?"

Carolyn looked away. She felt as though she couldn't breathe.

"I . . . I've got to go," she stammered.

Clah again smiled, crinkling the the corners of his eyes. "Yes, I suppose you do. Give my respects to your father. *Hágoóneé.*"

Carolyn grabbed her umbrella, dropped the almanac on a table, and rushed out of the library. The air outside cooled her and she took a deep breath. Thunder rumbled and the rain began. She unfurled the umbrella and skipped over a foaming gully, then crossed the street and headed across a parking lot. The large adobe-style courthouse loomed on her left. Glancing back at the library, she watched to see if Clah followed her. A man in a canvas raincoat ran from his car toward the library's double doors, shielding his head with a briefcase, but no one came out. She hurried away.

What was Clah doing at the library? Was he spying on her? And why would he seem so interested in what she was doing? He had certainly unnerved her; it was obvious he knew what she was doing there.

After maneuvering around several puddles, Carolyn realized that she didn't have the vaguest idea where she was going. She didn't know the name of her parents' attorney nor did she know where his office was located. The digital clock above a bank read three forty-five. Her parents would be on their way to pick her up.

Carolyn crossed another street, turned up a block, then walked quickly back toward the library. Cars passed, spraying her boots and jeans with the water that plumed from their tires. Although she was drenched, that didn't bother her nearly as much as Clah had. She trudged on, shielding herself beneath the umbrella.

She looked back and noted a black form coming in her direction, a block behind her. Carolyn walked faster. Was it Clah? She turned around again, feeling the rain against her face. The blur stopped moving and shifted backward in a way that reminded her of a giant roach ducking for cover.

For a moment, Carolyn felt lightheaded.

She crossed another intersection, trying to orient herself. She should be close to the library. A horn honked. Carolyn jumped back to the curb as a pickup zoomed past.

Panic rose to the surface. Again she turned around, but the dark figure behind her wasn't there. More cars flew past, sloshing her with muddy water. Another car honked and Carolyn jumped. It took a moment for her to realize that the silver-colored Jeep pulling off to the side of the road belonged to her parents. As the passenger window slid down, she saw her mother's face.

"Hop in. Hurry!"

The door opened, and Carolyn ducked into the back seat, slamming the door shut as the vehicle sped away from the curb. Her father's frown was reflected back at her in the rearview mirror. He was going to be demanding an explanation soon.

"Look at you. You're soaked!" her mother cried.

"It's nothing, really," Carolyn sputtered, feeling a rush of relief.

CHAPTER TWENTY-FIVE

The wind was fast and loud, beating against the building on two sides, its noise like banshee wails. It spoke with a thousand voices, whistling, shouting, rasping past cracks and corners. Carolyn crouched motionless in the darkness, waiting. She heard a soft rustle to her left and knew it was Jesse, was glad it was Jesse; she just wished she could see him. She sat there, more than ever aware of the wind's shrieking curses.

Peering through the open window, Carolyn looked up into the moonless night. The scale of the black bowl of the sky was littered with stars. She shivered. Glancing in Jesse's direction, she searched the darkness, wanting to call out to him for assurance.

The wind grew quiet.

At the same instant she heard something outside, a sound like a large animal running. Something was moving through the trees. Coming their way. Coming fast.

Suddenly the door flew open and she turned to see a large doglike figure commanding the doorway. Its paws were covered with ashes. A glare as evil as hell itself was in its eyes, and a low, almost inaudible growl came from its throat.

Carolyn tried to call out to Jesse but wasn't able.

She pulled herself into the corner shadows, cowering into a trembling, whimpering ball.

The animal didn't move. But as Carolyn watched, the dog became human, hooded in a wolf's skull and wearing a fur pelt over his shoulders. He stepped toward her, his mouth opening but not speaking. His soot-covered hands reached out to her, drawing closer and closer as the wind pounded through the room.

She backed away, groping against the wall, frantic. *Where was Jesse?*

And then she knew.

Terror-stricken, she turned to face the hovering animal, and now she could see him clearly, the blood encrusted claws, the ghastly face. She looked up into the malevolent eyes of Jesse Begay.

A scream rose in her throat, a scream cut short as she jerked awake and sat straight up in bed. Her heart raced; her breath came in short, shallow gasps.

Just a dream, she realized.

It was just a dream.

Tomorrow she had to find Jesse.

Tomorrow they had to put an end to this.

CHAPTER TWENTY-SIX

The following night there were no dreams. There was no sleep, only waiting. And finally, there was a light tap on the window: Carolyn's cue. She quietly swung her feet to the floor and sat on the edge of the bed, buttoning her jacket. She had gone to bed fully dressed so she would be ready when Jesse came. The floor creaked softly as she walked to the window and opened it. Outside, a heavy mist greeted her.

"Do you need a hand?" Jesse whispered, his breath a brief plume.

Carolyn shook her head. Using the half-open dresser drawer as a step, she hoisted herself up to the window sill, straddled it, then ducked through. Once outside and breathing hard, she quietly followed Jesse's dark shape as he moved away from the cottage, away from her sleeping parents, away from safety, toward the trading post parking lot.

In a way it was like walking through a dream, Carolyn thought. Or maybe a nightmare. The world was gone. Before her was a weightless gauze of dark silver that parted as she passed and re-formed behind her. It was a shimmering void in which all she could do was follow the figure a few feet in front of her.

She was about to call out for Jesse to wait when she saw the old pickup truck through the mist. Jesse climbed into the driver's seat and turned on the ignition and the headlights as Carolyn pulled open the passenger-side door. The truck's lights penetrated only as far as the nearest trees. Jesse tinkered with the radio as Carolyn scooted onto the seat. The raspy tune of an unfamiliar song crackled through the dashboard speaker before he switched it off. Shifting into first, he smiled at Carolyn as he speeded up and moved through the gears.

There wasn't a lot to say at this point. They watched the headlights cut the night mist as they bounced toward Harrison Chee's hogan. Boston, riding clubs, and school dances were of another world, Carolyn realized. She dug into her pocket for the ghost beads Harlan Mitchell had given her, comforted that she had them. That idea alone sparked a smile. Who would ever believe this?

She looked over at Jesse. He was wearing a black baseball cap, his thick hair hanging loose over his shoulders. He was calm, chewing on his bottom lip, watching the road, and acting like he knew precisely what to do. Their plan had been hatched earlier, when Jesse and his mom had stopped by the store. Carolyn had been able to pull Jesse away from the adults long enough to tell him about her encounter with Clah. She had also told him that tonight was the Dark Night. Jesse promised he would come for her later, as soon as it was safe to assume that her parents were sleeping.

The truck bumped along the rutted road, occasionally lurching on a slick spot where the mud hadn't dried from yesterday's rain. Carolyn stifled a yawn and tried to make out the hands on her watch. Too dark.

"Were you able to find anything else worth salvaging from the fire?" she asked in an effort to make conversation.

"As a matter of fact, yes," he replied. "Mom found her old chest full of her wedding stuff. It also had Dad's army uniform and medals in it. Nothing was damaged."

"That's great. Anything else?"

"Yeah. I dug around my studio area. There were a couple of sculpture pieces that weren't damaged too bad. There was one that I had just started that wasn't even charred."

"Good. What about your tools?"

"I haven't found any yet. They're going to bring the tractor over from the Chapter House tomorrow or the day after and just push all the rest of the stuff into a big hole. That'll be the end of it."

"Where are you going to live?"

"Mom says we'll be getting some money from the tribe. When we do, my uncle and some other relatives are coming over to help us build a small house."

"At the same place?"

Jesse shrugged. "Probably. It's our land. And we still have a corral there, and the sheds."

Carolyn nodded. It was funny. Here they were talking like after tonight their lives would just return to normal. But would they? Would she and Jesse even see tomorrow? Here they were, on their way to expose a real, live witch—something so wicked that it was capable of burning down homes and committing murder.

According to the crystal gazer, the skinwalker possessed powers far beyond those of humans. And then there were the Navajo stories about the *Yee naaldlooshii* being able to turn into a wolf or an owl. How were they going to stop the thing? It wasn't as though they really had some thought-out strategy about what to do if the creature did show itself tonight. Carolyn noted that she hadn't seen Jesse's rifle in the pickup when she got in, and she didn't know if she was glad for that or not: Guns scared her, but so did skinwalkers. If the witch kept his appointed rendezvous at Chee's, maybe she and Jesse would just throw dirt clods at him. That would surely scare away any skinwalker who knew what was good for him, she told herself sarcastically. God, what were they doing out here tonight?

"What are we going to tell your grandfather?" Carolyn said aloud, trying to dispel the anxiety settling over her. "Don't you think he's going to think you're a little old for slumber parties and a little too young for bringing home a bride?"

A tiny smile played on Jesse's lips. "Probably. But I doubt if he's going to be thinking much about anything tonight except his sheep. I talked him into staying up at my uncle's summer camp tonight so he could herd his sheep back down to our area tomorrow. They're overgrazed up there and need to come back. My uncle's been too sick to do it, and Mom and I have our hands full with cleaning up the mess from the fire. Mom's staying at Lena's, and I told her I wanted to stay with Grandfather. So lucky for us, we'll have the place to ourselves."

"Oh yeah, lucky for us. Lucky for the skinwalker,

too," Carolyn commented. "No witnesses to see us murdered."

Jesse grinned at her, his teeth gleaming in the dark. "True. We have the *Yee naaldlooshii* all to ourselves. Hopefully, he'll still show up. I made arrangements to get the old man up to my uncle's at the last minute, so I'm banking that the witch won't know my grandfather is gone. It'll be our little surprise."

"Do you think Clah is the skinwalker, or Tullie?"

After an awkward pause, Carolyn looked over at Jesse. He was holding back something, she was certain. She had a feeling that he had already figured out the witch's identity but was unwilling to tell her yet.

"What do we do when the skinwalker shows up?" she asked, deciding not to press him; she was sure it wouldn't do any good, anyway.

"Leave it to me—I think I know how to handle it."

She gave him a you've-gotta-be-kidding look and said, "Great. That makes me feel a whole lot better."

"Good. I'm glad you're so confident in me."

She managed a smile and Jesse grinned. But they could not forget where they were going or why, and their smiles faded into a pair of matching frowns. Jesse pulled the truck off the trail and parked, switching off the headlights before killing the engine. "We'll leave the truck here and walk the rest of the way. The hogan is just over the hill," he said, pointing off into the night.

Carolyn nodded. In the darkness of the cab, it was difficult to see Jesse, but she could sense a mixture of fear and anticipation. Feelings welled up inside her stronger than anything she'd ever felt before, strengthening her, suddenly making her realize that she could love this strange, brave, beautiful boy. She kissed him lightly, quickly, and got out of the truck.

Without looking back, Carolyn groped ahead, climbing a small knoll in the direction Jesse had pointed. She could hear his footsteps behind her. Suddenly a circle of light leapt to the right, then traveled along the ground until it engulfed her. She turned and faced the glare of Jesse's flashlight, shielding her eyes with her hand.

"Wait up," Jesse called to her.

The light bobbed up and down as he came closer.

"Here, I brought an extra," he said, handing her a flashlight of her own.

She flicked it on and swept the beam in front of her. A shaft of light swooped over the rocks and cut into the hazy forms of the trees before being swallowed up in the heavy mist. Ghosts swirled and danced inside the white column. Carolyn waved the beam from side to side, panning it across the half-hidden landscape. The red clay trail was steep and slick with rain, and more than once she nearly lost her footing. Jesse, more confident in his knowledge of the rugged terrain, led the way, occasionally stopping so that she could catch up. The temperature seemed to have dropped sharply, and the mist felt even colder to Carolyn than the chill of fear that was gripping her and growing with each step.

She saw Jesse fumble with a ring of keys as they approached an old hogan. A moment later, he pushed the door open warily and pointed his light inside.

"Here we are: home sweet home," he said softly. He disappeared inside, his flashlight beam dancing through the window. Carolyn followed him in, adding another ray of light to slide across the floor and walls.

The hogan was cluttered and dirty, she observed. Dishes were piled in a filthy basin atop the narrow counter; a cot covered with rumpled sheets and a stained blanket occupied one of the shadowed corners; a wooden chest squatted in another. A table with two mismatched chairs and a cracked vinyl couch fanned out at angles away from the cast-iron stove that dominated the center of the room. Several small windows bounced light back at her; some were cracked, all were dirty and unadorned with curtains.

"We'd better find places to get comfortable, then kill the lights," Jesse directed. "I'll take this side." Carolyn watched as he pulled a chair over to one of the windows, then clicked off his flashlight. She sat down on the creaking couch after checking for bugs or anything else that might be lying in wait. Snapping off her light, she stared into the void she had just created and was tempted to switch her light back on.

"Now what?" she whispered.

"Shhh. We wait."

Wait. Wait for what—to get murdered? Not much of a plan, Carolyn grumbled to herself, secretly hoping that no one showed up. She thought with longing of her bed, of sleep, of reading a book, propped against the blanket while a light kept her safe from the dark. Again, her fingers rubbed the ghost beads in her pocket. Jesse sat motionless nearby. Her nightmare came back to her, a little too vividly. *Déjà vu.* Waiting in the dark with Jesse Begay.

"Jesse?" she whispered.

Silence. Just like in her dream.

A knot of fear formed in her stomach.

"Jesse?"

Something moved.

Unable to stifle her fear, she clicked on her flashlight, stabbing the light toward Jesse. Reflexively, he shielded his eyes.

"What are you doing?"

Seeing the folly of her panic, Carolyn switched off her light. She heard Jesse swear under his breath and rustle around. Something about the scene suddenly struck her as funny. Trying to muffle this unexpected attack of the giggles, she cupped a hand over her mouth and snorted into it.

"What's so funny?" she heard Jesse whisper, sounding slightly annoyed. This only drew louder cackles.

"You're losing it," he said. "Crazy *bilagáana*." More giggles.

Carolyn could now hear Jesse trying to control his own amusement, which didn't help matters. Her body trembled, threatening to erupt with laughter. Suddenly a light reflected off Jesse's window, and the giggling stopped abruptly. Someone was coming. The rumble of an engine drifted through the night. As they listened, a pale glow moved through the darkness outside the window. Minutes stretched into hours; the engine stopped; a door slammed. Carolyn held her breath and waited.

It wasn't what she had expected: someone boldly driving up to Chee's hogan in a truck. But why not?

Impulsively, she crouched lower on the sofa, expecting all hell to break loose. Jesse's silhouette rose soundlessly from the chair and loomed in the pale wash of light. Carolyn clasped her ghost beads tightly and began to pray.

Outside Jesse's window, a blinding gyre of light bobbed and footsteps scuffled to the door. There was a knock. Carolyn pressed herself into the vinyl, willing herself invisible. Seconds later came another knock. Should they answer it? A skinwalker wouldn't come to the door with a flashlight and knock, would he? Somehow this wasn't what she had envisioned their confrontation would be like.

A voice called out.

A familiar voice pierced the silence. It called out again: "Chee? You home?" Another sharp rap on the door.

Clah.

More footsteps outside as he headed toward a window. Carolyn buried her head in her lap before the beam from Clah's light lanced through the glass, tracing a path to the table, over to the stove, across the floor inches from Jesse's feet, toward Chee's unmade bed. It rested there for a moment as another tap sounded on the windowpane. A pause, then footsteps returned to the door.

Carolyn's mind filled with questions. Would he come inside? What would she and Jesse tell him if he did? Certainly, he would demand an explanation of what they were doing here, hiding in the dark. But what was *he* doing here? Was Clah casing the place, only to return later as the skinwalker? Or had her suspicions been wrong? Was Clah their enemy, or had he come here to help? Should she answer the door? What was Jesse thinking?

She expected the door to swing open any second and Clah's blinding strobe to pounce on her, to interrogate her. A sick feeling swept through her as her heart thudded in her chest.

It took Carolyn a moment to realize that the footsteps were growing fainter, the light waning. Clah was leaving!

Welcome silence.

"Jesse?" she whispered.

"Shhh."

"He can't hear me."

A car door slammed. An engine revved, then slowed, then revved again, the sound of a vehicle reversing, then inching forward, then reversing again. Clah was turning around.

"I have to go to the bathroom," she announced, unabashed.

"Wait."

"I can't." She listened to Clah's vehicle as it crept away, growing fainter. "Jesse?"

"Okay. Here, follow me and keep your light off. There's an outhouse out back."

Carolyn cringed at the thought of using an outhouse, but the alternatives weren't to her liking either: She could either hold it all night or venture into the spiny bushes. No thanks. She stood up and followed his black shape out the door. The fog seemed denser, animated. Jesse took her hand and led her across the rough ground, giving permission for her to turn on her flashlight only when she entered the rickety outbuilding.

"So is Clah our witch?" she called out, hoping her

question drowned out the embarrassing sounds she was making.

Still no comment from Jesse.

Clicking off her light, she pushed open the door and again took his hand. "Now he knows your grandfather isn't here."

Jesse navigated her around several obstacles: a low pile of firewood, a metal drum, and a couple of old tires. "It doesn't matter. The *Yee naaldlooshii* will be here."

"What are you *not* telling me?"

"Nothing. I can't explain it."

"Try," Carolyn persisted. She would have stumbled into the side of Chee's hogan if Jesse hadn't cautioned her with a handsqueeze. Taking up their positions inside the dark hogan for a second time, Carolyn became slightly annoyed. "Okay. Let's hear it. What are you keeping from me?" she whispered.

"Nothing," Jesse answered. He hated to lie to her, but now wasn't the time for explanations. He now questioned his decision to bring Carolyn here with him. It wasn't fair to her; it was far too dangerous. Maybe he should have come alone. "Everything was meant to come to this," he murmured. "When the two of us meet, only one will walk away."

Carolyn sat in the pitch dark, musing over Jesse's words. It scared her. Whatever was going on here was much deeper than anything she was able to fathom. Something beyond logic, beyond Clah, beyond Tullie, beyond Jesse. It was as though some other forces were at war here: something primitive and foreign. She was merely a bystander.

Carolyn thought about it for a long time. Exhaustion wrapped its cloak about her more than once, gently wooing her toward sleep before she jerked herself awake again. It grew colder and quieter, until finally the mere weight of the silence threatened to crush her.

And then she knew the wolf had come.

She could feel its presence on the other side of the door.

The appointed hour had arrived.

CHAPTER TWENTY-SEVEN

The door to Chee's hogan blew open with the shock of a shotgun blast. Carolyn's scream lodged in her throat like a lump of gristle, threatening to choke the breath right out of her body. She stared at the figure in the doorway. Part man, part beast: It was the embodiment of her worst nightmare.

Silhouetted in the darkness was the figure of a man crowned with the head of a wolf.

In the thick gloom, eternity came in a thunderclap. Time folded in on itself, backward and forward, casting a spell on the shadowlands of her fear, on the mist-filled, moonless night. Evil surrounded the *Yee naaldlooshii*. Revulsion was the atmosphere he breathed, the air he pulled into his lungs, the life of his being. Carolyn shrank into her fear, paralyzed as a rabbit waiting to be torn apart by a wolf. The wolf stepped into Chee's hogan and focused on the cot. To her utter amazement, he didn't seem aware of her and Jesse hiding in the darkness. The beast moved in closer, silent and fluid. He came to an abrupt halt in the center of the room, finally sensing their presence. Cold seemed to come from him like winter's mist.

A sudden flick of a match illuminated Jesse in dark

halo. The wolf swung swiftly around; light reflected off metal: He held a knife. Jesse walked toward the table, bent down, lit the lantern's wick, and blew out the match. With apparent ease, he sat down behind the lamp and turned up the flame, casting shadows to the dark corners. As the glow filled the room, the musk of kerosene hung heavily in the air.

The boy's behavior was audacious—it was blasphemy. The wolf stood within striking distance; the light lined the edges of his long blade, and he actually seemed to grow larger. Carolyn could make out human features below the wolf's skull, although the face was covered with a crust of mud. The wolf finally glanced in her direction, and she looked into the cold emptiness of his eyes. Her skin crawled. There was something familiar about those eyes. . . .

He dismissed her as unimportant and again glowered at Jesse. They stared at each other for what seemed like an eternity, measuring and weighing.

Jesse's eyes stung from the lamp. Carolyn saw a hard smile play at the corners of his lips. There was no fear, obviously, only hatred. It was a Jesse she had never seen before, a Jesse that scared her almost as much as the beast in front of her.

"My grandfather isn't here," Jesse said.

The wolf's gaze traveled across the room. He jerked his head toward Carolyn, then back to Jesse; the forepaws of the animal skin moved across his shoulders. Slowly, he began to back toward the door. Mesmerized, Carolyn watched, sure that in a moment he would be gone, nothing more than the night's illusion.

"No need to rush off, Harlan," Jesse said. "We need to talk."

The wolf froze in his tracks. He raised the knife threateningly, pointing it at Jesse.

"It is you, isn't it, Harlan? Or do you lose yourself when you wear the death head of the *Yee naaldlooshii? Díkwíí báah ílí?* How much does it cost?"

"*Táá'altsogóó,*" a voice whispered. Everything.

Carolyn was dumbfounded. Harlan Mitchell? Could it be? She had believed the witch was Clah or Tullie. But Harlan Mitchell? Her fingers instinctively let go of the ghost beads and let them drop to the floor. "Harlan?"

In that instant Carolyn felt violence gather in the cold air that surrounded them and her heart nearly froze. He looked at her, malevolence gleaming.

"We need to talk," Jesse repeated.

The wolf's silence was thick with scorn. Finally he peeled the skull off his head, exposing short-cropped hair, a human profile. In spite of the mud-smeared face, it was indeed Harlan Mitchell. He dropped the wolfskin to the floor and straddled the chair across from Jesse, setting the knife on the table within reach.

"Why?" asked Jesse.

Harlan shrugged, tried to smile. "A joke. I was simply playing a joke on the old man. I'm no witch."

"You're lying."

Harlan wrung his hands. "Go to hell," he spat, his eyes wandering to the knife.

"You're already there. You've broken the greatest taboo of the Diné. You've defiled yourself. *Ha`atíibiniiy'e?* For what purpose?"

Harlan shook his head. "What are you talking about? I told you; I was playing a joke on Chee. I don't even believe in all that crap."

"You're lying," Jesse persisted, his voice betraying his deep emotion. "You're the *aditlgashii* and I'm here to destroy you."

Carolyn could see Harlan's muscles tighten beneath his shirt; he looked ready to leap over the table. Jesse stared at him, his jaw set, his eyes thin slits. Harlan diminished under the boy's gaze.

"Twilight Boy," he muttered matter-of-factly.

"*Aó,*" Jesse replied. "*Ei shí shízhí.*" It is my sacred warrior name, given to me by the *Yeibichei* under *Dook'o'oosliid*, the Sacred Mountain in the West."

"Yes," Harlan hissed. "I have seen you in the coals of my fires. I've pissed on the ashes of your image, Twilight Boy. You have no power over me. I could kill you as you sit there. You are nothing." Tension hung over the table as Carolyn looked on, trying to understand what was happening.

Jesse shook his head. "*Ndagá.* It's over. The wolf's teeth are shattered. Your name will never again be spoken. Soon you will join the ranks of the dead."

Harlan attempted to laugh. "You're a fool. You come with your self-righteous prattle about broken taboos and sacred names. You're not without blemish. Tell me about this *bilagáana* tramp you are with. You should stick to your own kind. She's not one of us . . . I should kill her."

Harlan turned his full attention on Carolyn, and she could feel the force of his glare as he held her contemptuously in his gaze. Her heart shrank in her chest. Harlan again dominated the room. Jesse, on the other hand, suddenly seemed less sure of himself, smaller. She looked away from Harlan's gaze.

Finally, Jesse snorted, "Go ahead. She means nothing to me."

She didn't hear that, Carolyn told herself. She wanted to get up and run away but her legs, her arms, her body were frozen—she couldn't move.

Harlan's mud-crusted face leered at her.

"I could throw her life away easily."

Jesse shrugged. "Do as you want with her. The *bilagáana* served her purpose. But your sorcery is broken."

Harlan's gaze returned to Jesse. The boy's words seemed to tear away chunks of his confidence. Anger faded from his eyes like the last embers of a wind-whipped fire. Harlan rubbed his hands over his face wearily, an unconscious gesture that broke away some of the clay.

Suddenly sitting before Carolyn was a tired old man, drained of the fearsome aura that had been present only a moment ago. Jesse looked up at her, and she could read the love there, could feel it like a blanket of warmth and comfort. He loved her. And then she understood.

The skinwalker's greatest source of power was the fear others had of him. Jesse had exposed him, but the skinwalker's retaliation had been the threat on Carolyn's life, the weak link in Jesse's armor, because of his feelings for her. If Harlan had been able to break Jesse's hold on him by threatening her, he could have destroyed them both.

Jesse pulled off his necklace and dropped the heavy coin onto the table. The clink of metal caused Harlan to look over; his hooded eyes stared coldly at the gold piece. "Tell me about the coins," Jesse commanded, his voice taut as piano wire. Harlan glanced down at his boots, shoulders hunched, hands folded. He shook his head. "The coins belong to the Dead."

The subsequent pause suggested that Harlan's explanation was finished.

Jesse reached over and took the coin in his hand, squeezing it so tightly that his knuckles turned white. When he spoke, there was a thick sound to his voice, emotion barely controlled. "I know that. Tell me about my father's death. I demand it. The hours of the Wolf are numbered, Harlan. I need to know what the coins have to do with my father."

"And what is *my* gain?"

It was clear that Harlan Mitchell hoped to strike some kind of deal with Jesse. A sly smile curled his upper lip, and he looked to Carolyn like a snarling dog.

"You can go to your grave with a clear conscience."

Harlan laughed. A coarse cackle. "The simple reasoning of youth. So naive. So cliché. I will tell you what you wish to know, Twilight Boy, simply for my own amusement. *Yisínists'áá*. But tell me, how did you learn the identity of the Wolf?"

"Your boots. At the trading post, when I was getting cigarettes for the crystal gazer, I noticed your boots. The size, the rounded toe. It made me start wondering. Later, I thought about the way you had ridiculed Desbah Yazzie, the bitterness in your voice when you spoke of the old woman. You knew she could harm you. And then later, there was the fire . . . My home burned to the ground shortly after our conversation that day, shortly after you learned that I had gone to see the crystal gazer." Jesse shrugged. "It added up."

"Perceptive," Harlan complimented. "You've meddled to the point of catastrophe. I'm impressed with your powers of deduction. Your father would be proud."

Carolyn found it amazing the many roles Harlan Mitchell could play. He now assumed the persona of a caring grandfather. She almost felt sorry for him until she remembered that only a moment ago he had threatened to murder her. The man changed like a chameleon.

Harlan tented his fingers, pressed his palms together, and stared intently into the lantern's flame. The dancing light reflected in his eyes. "I have devoted my life to the dark secrets of the *Yee naaldlooshii*. I have gained powers unknown to the uninitiated. I have become one with the night: the dark, the owl, the wolf. My power is great."

Just as quickly as before, Harlan's expression changed. He glared at Carolyn. She tried to swallow the lump in her throat. She felt she was in a room with a rabid dog whose chain was almost long enough for him to reach her. Jesse, on the other hand, seemed indifferent, aloof. "Tell me about these coins," he said, tossing the gold piece back onto the table. "How did my father end up with this?"

"Ask your grandfather; they belong to him," Harlan snarled.

"I'm asking you, the Wolf. Tell me all you know, Harlan. Let me see through your eyes, just for a moment."

"That would be dangerous, Twilight Boy. Dark waters run deep."

"I can swim."

Harlan chuckled. "Your brashness deserves humoring. You're an impetuous boy; you're a lot like your dad."

"And you're a monster," Jesse countered. "You've fed off the fear of others, creating terror, just to gain the power you crave."

Harlan made a mock bow.

Carolyn realized with a shudder that at this moment these two enemies were admiring each other. Each acted as if his goal was to win the other's applause, the other's approval.

"Tell me about the coins," Jesse persisted.

"And where should I begin?" Harlan asked, a sneer again twisting his mouth. "Should I tell you of the treachery I saw in my fires? Of the greed between two Spanish soldiers long ago? Should I tell you of the dagger that is buried in the bones of one of them? Or would you care to learn about the arrow that later pierced the breast of the remaining thief? I've seen it all in countless fires: how the gold lay unspoiled for many years in a shallow grotto where the *chindi* slept until awakened by two foolish boys. I've seen it all.

"Long ago I knew your grandfather. I roomed with his younger brother at boarding school. Tyrone and I were friends. The very night he returned to the dormitory after running away, he gave me his handful of coins. Tyrone didn't want them; he was afraid. He never told Chee that he had disclosed their secret to me, or that he had given away the coins.

"After Tyrone died, Chee became a wreck. I tried to comfort him, but it was like befriending a fencepost.

There was no response from Chee. I tried to gain his confidence, tried to coax him into talking about his trip across the mesas, but he refused. In the late spring, I told Chee he had mourned long enough, that it was time to go on with his life. I also told him that Tyrone had confided in me about the gold coins; I suggested that we become partners and retrieve the treasure. Chee, of course, refused. He said the coins belonged to the Dead, and he swore he would never again speak of them.

"So I remained poor, yet with a knowledge that a fortune in gold was scattered across the bones of the dead, somewhere between Waterless Mesa and Red Butte. I searched but found nothing. I searched again and again, combing the rocks and canyons, praying to find the hollow that Chee and Tyrone had stumbled upon. Needless to say, my efforts were in vain. Chee kept his promise of never returning to the coins. Years passed. I moved away but came back to Diné Bakiyah many years later. Chee had married, had kids, your mother for one. I ran into him at a ceremony in Window Rock in '63, but he didn't even remember me even after I introduced myself. Chee's past was already well buried.

"But seeing him awakened the ache in my soul. I began to look to the spirit world for guidance. I searched the ancient ways, the old religion. I learned of the Hopi sorcerers, the powerful *Ya-Ya* ceremonies, and, later, the witchcraft of my own people. I sought out those who were learned in such medicine on the reservation, an almost impossible task: Their lives are surrounded in secrecy. I devoted my life to the dark secrets of the *Yee naaldlooshii* and gained powers unknown and unfathomed by the uninitiated. I became one with the night, the dark, the wolf. My power is great.

"As my power grew through the years, I was able to see the lost treasure in my fires, but its pathway remained hidden. I developed a plan that would force Chee to lead me to the gold."

"What kind of plan?" Jesse queried. Carolyn was forgotten by both of them. The past held more power than the present.

Harlan bared his teeth in a smile. "If Chee believed he had to return the coins he had buried with Tyrone, it would force him to shake off his years of idleness and help me retrieve what should be mine. I began leaving my little tokens on the old fool's doorstep over a year ago, hoping to scare the information out of him. Fear is a good reminder of things past. I had learned that Chee's wife had died, and that his drinking was getting worse. I had no idea how much time I had before his memory gave out altogether, if it hadn't already. I knew I was running out of time. I placed one of Tyrone's coins at Chee's door, then returned a month later with another. Your father's coin was to be the third."

Jesse leaned, listening intently.

"Apparently, Chee told your father about the reappearance of what he believed were the coins he had placed in Tyrone's coffin. I really hadn't expected him to tell anyone. By the third coin I grew careless. I parked my truck within a half-mile of Chee's hogan and dropped off the coin just as before. It was around midnight. Your father must have been staked out nearby, waiting for me. I didn't figure out for some time how he knew I'd be there that night. But what I realized later was that I made both of my earlier visits on the nights with no moon, it must have been instinctive. I wasn't even aware of it at the time. I'll hand it to Franklin Begay: He was a smart cop.

"Franklin must have picked up the coin before coming after me. I fled with him following at my heels. I thought I had lost him by the time I made it to my truck, but within minutes after pulling away, I saw headlights in my rearview mirror. This led to a high-speed chase past Whippoorwill Springs and White Rock. Your father lost control of his vehicle near the washout at Salt Creek; his truck went off the road and rolled several times. This, of course, I found out the following day. All I realized that night was that the headlights pursuing me had vanished. I assumed he had merely given up the chase. Franklin Begay was another fatality tied to the Coins of the Dead."

Carolyn watched Jesse wipe his eyes with the palm of his hand. "I blame you for his death," he said. "If it weren't for you, he would still be alive. You killed him."

Harlan stared at Jesse, but said nothing. There was no remorse, no understanding of Jesse's grief. He continued: "After Franklin's death, I had to wait until things settled down before resuming my visits to Chee. My next social call came the night I burned down his brush arbor. I appeared at his bedside a week later. Chee was finally ready to follow me to hell, if need be."

Jesse shook his head. "I doubt if he could even remember where the gold is. And if he did, what would you have done with him afterward, kill him?"

Harlan didn't answer the question. "He knows the pathway leading to the Dead."

209

"I doubt it. Whiskey and grief have destroyed his mind. He would have led you nowhere."

Harlan smiled wryly. "No, Twilight Boy, you're wrong. Tonight the gold would have been mine, if you had stayed out of things. I saw the treasure in my fires, but I also knew I had a nemesis. I knew of you, Twilight Boy. I wish you had died in the fire I gave you. Again, more meddling. I should also have snuffed out the life of that old medicine woman years ago."

Carolyn was chilled by the casualness with which Harlan Mitchell talked about killing. Here was a man with no conscience, no respect for life, no concept of right and wrong beyond what benefited him. She had read about people like this, but this was the first time she had actually seen one, listened to one, shared the same air that one breathed. She shuddered. Sitting within feet of her was a rabid animal capable of killing her and Jesse and walking away without the slightest remorse for what he'd done.

Harlan Mitchell suddenly stood up. His figure loomed threateningly in the shadows. Jesse kicked back his chair and moved toward the door, blocking the man's escape. Carolyn stood up also, unsure of what to do. Suddenly she heard a faint rumble, the sound of a vehicle approaching.

"I'll be going now," Harlan said casually. "That will be that nosy cop of yours, sniffing around again. You can thank him for saving your pitiful little lives."

"Stay," Jesse commanded.

"For what? What do you think happens next, Twilight Boy? Am I to give myself up? Or am I to lie down and whither before your eyes? You have indeed exposed me, but my powers aren't yet broken."

Harlan Mitchell reached up and snapped his fingers. The light from the lantern dimmed for a second, then flickered out; the room was suddenly as dark as a mine shaft. Carolyn instinctively crouched, heard the sound of something like wingbeats through the blackness. The room had shifted into night, and she was in the dark with a killer.

Carolyn felt violence gather in the dead air. She heard the rustle of clothing—Jesse must have moved away from the door. The wolf was going to kill her, she knew, and all she could do was crouch and wait.

A low voice whispered an incantation, then she heard the snap of a match. A tiny flame bloomed, floated in the darkness to the lantern. A moment later the room was once again awash in light. Jesse blew out the match.

She and Jesse were amazed to find that Harlan Mitchell had vanished.

CHAPTER TWENTY-EIGHT

Grabbing the knife off the table, Jesse rushed out the door. Carolyn followed at his heels with her flashlight. There was no sign of Harlan, but headlights from Clah's truck sliced through the mist. Jesse took the lead in a wild dash through the darkness, turning once, twice, then again. They climbed upward, gradually at first, then more steeply. Carolyn concentrated on keeping sight of Jesse's figure while trying not to trip. The white disk of her light stretched and widened along the rocky surface. She ran on, her lungs burning, her heart hammering in her chest. Breath caught and tore. Jesse seemed sure of where they were going.

He stopped, turned his head sideways, listening for something, giving Carolyn the opportunity to catch up. "Be careful," she said, whispering the obvious when she was finally close enough. Her breath swirled in front of her.

Jesse nodded, panting hard. He pointed up ahead, then started off again, leaving Carolyn no alternative but to try to keep up. As she ran, forms swam out of the dark, reaching for her; each veil of mist pulsed with danger. Jesse slowed as the terrain grew more rugged. "Careful," she said again, as if saying it made things safer.

Suddenly Jesse stopped and motioned her to silence.

Their lights skipped over large boulders and across gnarled trees. Then she heard it: the sound of a small rock slide as someone ran ahead of them on the trail. Jesse started off at once. Carolyn stifled her impulse to call out a caution once again.

A scream that could have raised the dead came down from above them and caused Jesse and Carolyn to again stop in their tracks. Carolyn's hand was shaking, the flashlight bounced its beam.

"What was that?" she asked, though she was sure she knew.

"The wolf. Come on!"

Scrambling over boulders, they followed the scream. Branches reached out for them like long, bony fingers. Below and to her left, Carolyn could see sheer blackness. A cliff. How far down it dropped she could only imagine; she didn't want to think about it. Panting made her throat raw; her lungs ached and her ears rang. She knew she was at the end of her endurance. She was about to call out to Jesse when she heard a gasp. The hair stood up on the back of her neck. Something bad was about to happen.

At the edge of her light beam stood the tall figure of Harlan Mitchell, shrouded once again in the wolf skin. He slowly turned around and faced them. The skull atop his head howled silently into the night.

Carolyn caught up with Jesse, keeping her light fixed on the wolf.

Harlan Mitchell looked strangely distorted. Sweat ran down his face, cutting thin trails through what remained of the mud. His eyes blinked against the light. He held up a hand to shield them from the glare, cursing.

The beam from her flashlight faded, as though the darkness of the wolf's soul had swallowed it. Carolyn rattled the light helplessly as it shrank to a dim glow. Jesse and Carolyn cautiously crept forward.

"Don't come any closer," his voice growled, venomously.

Carolyn felt her feet fuse to the rocks, knees locked, paralyzed by the command. Fear once again penetrated every muscle. As Harlan Mitchell had declared, his powers were far from broken. Jesse stood within reach, also immobilized.

There was a low laughter of triumph.

"Do you hear the Dead?" he called out.

They looked at each other. There was no sound except for the short panting of their own breathing.

"Their voices are calling me. Music from their mouths are calling me. Can you hear them?" Harlan Mitchell laughed again, a spewing noise that sounded almost obscene. "No man is immortal. *Hágoóneé.*"

By some trick, Harlan disappeared, as if swallowed by the earth. Another illusion. Harlan Mitchell, the master deceiver. Carolyn started to run forward but felt strong hands grasp her arms, yanking her back, pulling her downward. In that instant she realized that she was within inches of a precipice, a fathomless void. She balanced briefly at the edge of hell before falling backward, landing hard on rock.

"My God!" she gasped. "He . . ."

Jesse pulled her to him as she sobbed convulsively. He held her tight, her face buried against his chest, and the mist closed in around them.

CHAPTER TWENTY-NINE

It was almost noon as Carolyn watched the Boeing 737 taxi to its terminal gate ten minutes later than scheduled. She peered through the heavy airport glass, squinting against the sun's reflection off the aircraft's polished metal, hoping to catch a glimpse of Thomas. Could he see her? A knot of excitement caused her to bounce on her tiptoes.

She caught a glimpse of herself mirrored in the glass and smiled. She looked good, she knew. Her hair was pulled back and clipped with a gold clasp; she was well turned out in tennis whites that contrasted with the black Stetson she wore, Thomas's farcical gift.

The plane crept closer, and Carolyn's patience was pushed to the limit. Heat reflected off the runway in watery ripples. On a day like today, Carolyn found it almost impossible to imagine the events of that mist-filled night only three days ago, the Night of the Wolf, as she and Jesse now called it. It almost seemed too disconnected with reality to have ever really occurred.

They had made it back to her house before daylight, accompanied by Officer Clah. Her mom was just putting on her first pot of coffee, and the look on her face the moment they walked in would stay with Carolyn for a long time. It was the look, Carolyn supposed, that only a mother could have, especially a mother who thought her child was safely in bed but found out otherwise. Her father had greeted her with a puzzled expression, brows knitted, eyes moving from Carolyn to Clah, to Jesse, and then back to Carolyn, awaiting an explanation.

Not sure of how or where to begin, Carolyn had finally erupted with the whole story: about the coins, about Harrison Chee's appointed night with the skin-walker, the appearance of the wolf, Harlan Mitchell's story, and his horrible end. It was a tangled and fragmented tale. Jesse had listened and nodded, Clah had scribbled down a few more notes, but he had already heard it once since finding them at Chee's hogan. Clah had been there, trying to make sense of the empty room with the open door and lighted lamp, when she and Jesse had returned. After hearing what they had to say, he followed them back up to the ledge where Harlan Mitchell had disappeared. He scanned the canyon floor with his light but to no avail: There was no sign of Harlan. Clah radioed in to his dispatcher and requested that an ambulance and rescue team meet him at Red Rock Trading Post by daybreak. It was too dangerous to search at night, he said: The terrain was too treacherous.

Her mom still held her first cup of coffee as Carolyn finished her story; it quivered in her hands. Her father shook his head in amazement, his face darkening with anger. He questioned Clah as to how much he knew about Harlan Mitchell. Clah had said that he knew nothing about the man and had never had any reason to investigate him. Clah then asked Carolyn and Jesse a few more questions and listened quietly, scratching down brief notes. Carolyn had expected Clah's usual cynicism but was surprised to find him polite. She didn't mention anything about her earlier suspicions of him being the skinwalker. Clah had questioned Jesse in Navajo, and Jesse had answered in terse replies in the same tongue. He handed Clah the wooden-handled knife he had taken off the table, the only solid piece of evidence in their possession.

Another police officer arrived, and Clah accompanied him out to the rescue team that had just pulled into the parking lot. They searched the ravine later that morning but, as Carolyn had half expected, didn't find anything: no body, no sign of Harlan Mitchell anywhere. Around noon she and Jesse had to go down to the police station and write out their accounts of what had happened. Carolyn found this difficult since it was hard for her to correlate time with specific details. Although she had been wearing a watch, she couldn't recall looking at it after she had climbed out of her window that night. Time had seemed completely disconnected from the events that followed.

Her parents grounded her for slipping off at night without telling them anything, but their relief at her safety had overcome any real anger. Being grounded was sort of a joke anyway—it wasn't like she had places to go to at Red Rock. She had been happy to stay home, groom Nakai, and ride him around in the stable out back. Nakai was restless, but Carolyn was more than content to stay within her confines. And although she was homebound, her parents had made the exception of letting her go to Albuquerque to see Thomas. Her father drove her and at that moment sat with a menu in the airport restaurant, giving Carolyn an opportunity for a brief visit with Thomas more or less in privacy.

The plane came to a halt, and the door swung open, meeting the jetway that unfolded out like an accordion. A voice came over the intercom announcing the arrival of Flight 104, asking for those boarding the plane for the continued flight to San Diego to please wait until all passengers had disembarked. Carolyn nervously brushed a loose strand of hair away from her eyes and waited. Butterflies flitted inside as her excitement mounted, mixed with other feelings.

She had only seen Jesse once since the Night of the Wolf. He had stopped by the store with his mom afterward, purchasing a small cartload of food. Carolyn found out that he had told his mother about Harlan Mitchell and about the events leading up to Franklin Begay's death. Jesse said that although his mother had cried, it had seemed to put a lot of her questions and doubts to rest. He also told Carolyn that relatives were building them a new home and that he was helping with the carpentry. Thinking of Jesse caused her to miss him.

Carolyn pushed her mind in another direction. She had discovered that people were not always what they seemed to be: Clah and Tullie, for instance. Both had aroused her suspicions. Clah's cynical manner at the police station and his indirect warning in the library had unnerved her, causing her to distrust him. She wondered now if it had been Clah following her after she had left the library that day in the rain, or if it had been Harlan Mitchell. And Tullie's surliness and overt disliking of her was another matter. She actually felt sorry for him now. What did she signify to him to elicit such an emotion? Was it her youth? Her confidence? Her ability to make friends? Was she a threat to him? Or did he simply hate her because she was a *bilagáana,* an interloper? Could those feelings be turned around? It was something she could work toward. Her mother had often said that a warm smile and a friendly gesture could thaw the coldest of hearts. Well, she certainly had an opportunity to test that theory on the coldest heart she had ever encountered.

And Harlan. The memory of him made her want to cry. He had seemed so noble, and there *had* been that side to him. Who could have ever guessed that within his soul grew a rot, nurtured and fed for years by greed and lust for power? Carolyn couldn't help but regret all that Harlan might have been able to offer had he not chosen the path of witchcraft. What a shame. What a waste.

People began filing through the gate, some looking for loved ones, others searching for the overhead screens with terminal information. They appeared in clumps: a cluster of people, then a gap, then another cluster. Carolyn grew more and more impatient, fidgeting with her hair, pushing her glasses up. Either Thomas had missed his flight or he was caught behind an open door to the john, waiting to be rescued by an observant flight attendant. Another cluster of people: two small children clutching the hands of a weary-looking mother; a balding man in a suit and tie. Another gap. Thomas.

He smiled and waved. Carolyn tipped her hat, cowboy-style, then waded though people to greet him. He looked gorgeous: tall, deeply tanned, dressed in a yellow silk shirt, khaki shorts, and hiking boots. His sun-bleached hair was longer than Carolyn had ever seen it before.

He greeted her with a kiss on the cheek. Carolyn squeezed his hand and smiled up into his blue eyes as she led him toward the empty row of chairs at the deserted corner of the terminal.

"Nice hat," Thomas said, allowing her to pull him along. Carolyn lightly pushed him into a chair and sat down next to him, still holding his hand, their knees touching. He teasingly tapped her on the brim of her hat. "So how's my cowgirl?"

Carolyn adjusted the Stetson. "Have you missed me?"

"You bet. Wish I could steal you away from here, take you to California with me. You look great." Carolyn blushed.

"Really. Get you in a swimsuit and California girls would have nothing on you."

She beamed at him but felt a tinge of uneasiness over his compliment.

"I missed you too," she lied. Actually, she had had little time to even *think* of him, except for this week, and then it had been difficult to remember exactly what he looked like.

"How have you been?" he asked. Before she could reply, he shook his head soberly. "Man, you've missed some fantastic parties. Since school's been out, it's been serious party time. You know Randy Edwards? Just last week we had a party at his place. His parents were out of town for the weekend, and I'll tell you, you wouldn't believe what went on over there. I heard the damage was in the thousands. The CD player ended up in the toilet. I guess an antique lamp got thrashed. Someone broke into his old man's wine cellar and scarfed down a couple bottles of vintage Merlot. I heard his parents were so angry that Randy was put on yard duty for the summer. A couple of us called over there, asking him if he'd come over and mow our lawns."

Carolyn missed the humor as she pictured Randy's parents coming home to a disaster.

"I told you about my cousin getting married, didn't I? The wedding's not until next week so we'll have plenty of time to do some last minute partying. I guess his fiancée's parents are taking care of everything; all he has to do is show up on the right day wearing a tux. The guy got a brand-new Corvette from his dad because he promised to finish college—what a bribe! We'll probably be at the beach every day. There's some bad-looking dune buggies down there, not to mention all the whacky types that hang out around the beach. Man, it makes Boston look like a whole different planet."

Carolyn nodded, feeling she was little more than an audience.

"After high school I'm moving out there. Boston's great, but the West Coast is where it's happening. My dad already told me he'd finance my tuition for Berkeley, but of course I'm hoping to get a scholarship in football. I met with Coach Stevens the day after school got out. I guess he's pretty impressed with what he saw last year—he just about promised me I'd be first-string quarterback. A lot of guys are going to be jealous that he gave it to a sophomore, but I'll be showing them why."

Thomas finally seemed to notice Carolyn's waning

attention. "So how's life in the boonies? I see you haven't been scalped yet. I'll never understand what got into your old man to pull a stunt like moving out to an Indian reservation. It's not fair to you."

Carolyn tried to smile, but couldn't get beyond a brief upward turn at the corners of her lips.

"Jeez, what's it like living out there? You must be bored out of your mind." He shook his head sympathetically. "Excitement probably centers around Friday night bingo games, huh? I have an aunt in Michigan who's always out playing bingo on the Indian reservation up there. Yep, that's what I want to do with my weekends," he said sarcastically. "Is there anyone out there to even talk to?"

"Yeah, there is *someone,*" she answered cryptically. "The Navajos I know are real easy to talk to. Matter of fact, they're pretty good listeners too."

Thomas nodded, giving no hint that he was aware he'd just been zinged.

"That's cool. I'm for the Indians. I mean, I've seen *Dances With Wolves* and *The Last of the Mohicans.* They're great flicks. You ever see that T-shirt with all the arrows painted on it? On the back it says, 'Custer's Last T-shirt.'" Thomas chuckled. "I'd like to get one—not that I'd ever wear it. Maybe I could give it to your old man."

Carolyn smiled as if she were amused, stifling the urge to look at her watch.

"Hey, you're awfully quiet. What's the matter . . . cat got your tongue? What teacher used to always say that? Jeez, used to drive me crazy. I mean, what a weird expression: Imagine some grungy ol' tom, hair all frizzed out like its tail was stuck in a socket, pawing on your tongue."

Thomas faked a dramatic shudder, finally getting a response from Carolyn. She laughed. "Mrs. Crawford. She always says that. She always tells Janet Freeberg that 'an idle mind is the devil's workshop.' We'd try not to laugh out loud, especially when Janet would roll her eyes as soon as Mrs. Crawford turned around. It was pretty funny."

Thomas grinned, trying to see the humor, or maybe just trying to focus on what Carolyn had said. The same crackly voice came over the intercom again, announcing the final boarding of Flight 104 for San Diego. Thomas stood up, pulling on Carolyn's hand. "Come on. Walk me to the gate."

At the boarding ramp, they stopped and faced one another; Carolyn slid her hand out of Thomas's loose grip. He beamed his most charming smile at her, eyes sparkling like a clear morning sky.

"Short and sweet, huh? I'll send you a postcard from San Diego." Carolyn nodded, feeling some regret that she hadn't tried harder during their brief encounter. "Well, I'll see you in August then," he said, bending over to give her a kiss. She offered her cheek, trying not to seem too obvious. Thomas pecked her lightly, then backed away though the gate, which was deserted now except for a smiling, impatient-looking flight attendant. "See you in August, cowgirl," he said, misreading the reason for her tears as he waved good-bye.

Carolyn smiled thinly and waved back, knowing at that moment she would not be seeing him in August, would possibly never see him again, and it didn't really matter.

CHAPTER THIRTY

Dawn began like every dawn; *Jóhonaa`eí* the Sun Carrier brightened the eastern horizon, blending mauve into cerulean, ensuring the continuity of life. For *Jóhonaa`eí* always returned with a single turquoise jewel called Sky. *Yá´doolt izh.*

Jesse began sanding the four-foot-high piece of stone with a torn scrap of emery cloth, fusing detail into abstract form. The curving shape represented a *Yei,* one of the First People, the Holy Ones who dwelled on the sacred mountains. It was to be his gift to Carolyn.

In this piece, Jesse intended perfect *hózhó*—harmony and beauty—for this was the Blessing Way. *Hózhó* was the goal of all living beings, including the earth, the mountains, and even the very stones under the teeth of his chisel. They all had both inner and outer forms; to achieve well-being, the inner forms must harmonize with *sá a naghai* and the outer forms must unify with *bikeh hózhó.* This was the gift to the Diné, as it was meant to be.

He realized he would not be able to explain all this to Carolyn, but that didn't matter. This would be her gift.

As he watched *Jóhonaa`eí* spread his arms across the eastern expanse of mesas, the crisp morning air sent a single shiver up his spine. It was invigorating.

His mind and heart were finally at peace. He had learned much during the past couple of weeks. He had learned that love was strength, that memories of his father were sacred. At first, Harlan Mitchell's story had haunted him at night, had caused him to wonder *what if,* just what if his grandfather had never discovered the lost gold on that snowy morning many years ago? How different his life would be now. His father would be alive, his mother would be happy, and he'd be a very different person—less serious, lighter of heart, maybe.

He learned that greed sowed destruction. He learned that believing in oneself brought singleness of purpose, that power was fleeting, that wisdom dwelt in the old ways. And now, maybe his father's death hadn't been totally in vain: His grandfather could live out his years in peace, the *chindi* put to rest, the witchcraft destroyed.

He rubbed the abrasive cloth lightly across the sculpture, feeling for irregularities in the surface, all the while casting glances toward the hogan. His grandfather was a light sleeper, and Jesse had been on the receiving end of the old man's wrath more than once this past week for waking him. He'd be glad when their new home was finished: no more creeping around in the mornings like a thief, no more hearing his grandfather's snoring. Sleeping on sheepskins thrown on the floor wasn't the most comfortable, either.

Teddy looked up from his mat near the doorstep, immediately wagging his tail and expecting attention. When it wasn't forthcoming, he dropped his snout to his forepaws and resumed his nap.

Jesse returned his attention to the sculpture, running a hand over the grainy surface, feeling, exploring.

Last night he had finally had the chance to share with his grandfather all that he had come to know about the gold coins. He told him the entire story: of Harlan Mitchell's greed, which led to the death of his father, and finally about the *Yee naaldlooshii*. It had been difficult for Jesse to read the old man's feelings. His grandfather hadn't responded, but he had listened. His eyes studied the emptiness between Jesse and himself, and he nodded ever so slightly, confirming that he heard. As Jesse had suspected, after he questioned his grandfather about the whereabouts of the treasure, Chee had mumbled something about not remembering where the *chindi*'s lair lay. All Jesse could get from him was an "out there" wave of indifference. His grandfather had waved in the general direction of Santa Fe. Or Chicago. Or Paris.

It would be impossible to convince his grandfather that Tyrone's death hadn't been his fault. The old man had cultivated his guilt for years, and he wasn't willing to share the blame.

Jesse wondered about Harlan Mitchell too. A body still hadn't been recovered from the chasm floor. He had been tempted to go and search himself, but something stopped him. Was it fear of *chindi*? He told himself it was the conviction that his part in the circle was finished. Besides, if Clah couldn't find a body, what made him think he could do better? Was it the fact that he knew Clah was looking for the corpse of a man? Jesse would search for an animal, a wolf. And maybe he wouldn't find anything either.

The great golden disk climbed upward ever so slowly, seeming to become caught in the tree branches. Its rays made a soft web of light and shadows. Jesse's thoughts turned to Carolyn.

She had been brave and tough throughout the entire ordeal. A person with less strength could have easily been shattered after their experiences with Harlan. One day soon he would drive over to the trading post and drop off his gift. Who knows? He might even propose that he and Carolyn take Nakai out for a spin, riding double. He knew of a great place where medicine men of old had painted an entire rock wall with fantastic pictures: graceful, elongated horses prancing across a shelf of rock.

He could show it to her and she'd respond with a smile like sunshine. And then, of course, there was El Morro: Inscription Rock. They could go there and read the names and dates that the Spaniards had carved into the soft sandstone. Maybe one of them had carried a fortune in gold coins to a small grotto near Waterless Mesa, and, once there, had kept a rendezvous with death. Maybe part of the secret could be found on the rock, written in stone.

ABOUT THE AUTHOR

Courtesy of Ray Evanger

Timothy Green, born in 1953 in Flint, Michigan, pursued various interests—world travel, art history, painting, and sculpture—before turning seriously to writing. He is the author of four works of fiction, including *Mystery of Navajo Moon* from Northland Publishing. He lives on the Navajo Reservation with his wife and two daughters.